Vampire Redemption

A COSMIC JOURNEY

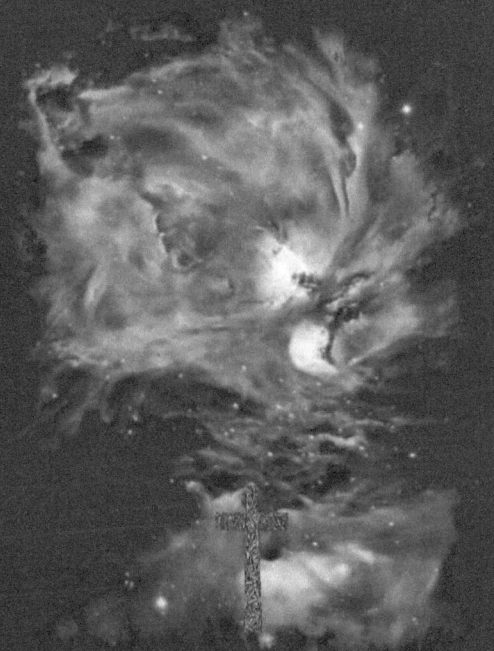

Steve H Hakes

Vampire Redemption

A Cosmic Journey

Steve H Hakes

Paperback ISBN: 978-0-9957013-7-3

Hardback ISBN: 979-8-4172990-7-0

Kindle ISBN: 978-0-9957013-6-6

V250813150048:   simbolinian@outlook.com

Thanks to...

- Sheridan Le Fanu's non-lesbian, *Carmilla* (1872)
- Christian songwriter/vampire writer, Sabine Baring-Gould's, *Margery of Quether* (1891)
- Bram Stoker's folk-Catholic, *Dracula* (1897)

War Unwanted

Vampires were watching. The war was over. No one had won except Overlord Ainet of Central Command, APOC (Artificially Pansophic Overall Centre). It had been a radiation war, no viruses, no chemicals, but a few big bangs over the biggest of the megalopoli, megacities created to efficiently relocate human populations.

It could have been worse, and fortunately had been waged long after technology was in place to detoxify the environment from radio-isotope clouds. These detox systems were self-sustaining, run by dumb computers isolated from the outside world, even from Central Command, and thus were perfectly secure. They would run and run and run, until they no longer detected any deadly rays in the atmosphere. Only then would they hibernate back into their long sleep of vigilance.

They had begun life asleep. No one had really expected that their slumber would be disturbed, but given the unexpected war, thank God that they had awoken. No, even thanking God remained politically unsafe: big boys behind big governments had put us right about that long ago. It was safer to thank the forgotten people of the forgotten past who had invested trillions into building them. Likely enough they would have been rubbished like Noah.

Noah? Few had heard of that name nowadays, and you could only find it in the Roman Files or some copies of ancient 'books'—books using an old way of transmitting information by material, but explanation is pointless. In days when people used 'money' to obtain things—it is pointless to explain all of the old customs—a very few at the top had been called trillionaires. Disturbing dreams had come to one of these elite, Baryshnya Anastasia Orakul. She in turn had inspired others of these superrich into protecting against the outside chance of a global radiation flood—hence the detoxers. But trillionaires had been influential in bad as well as in good ways. They had given their worldviews to Ainet, ideas that human beings could be valued according to a net financial worth, thoughtlessly raising the Sword of Damocles over rich and poor alike.

Nevertheless, based on the fears of the few, detoxifiers had been built to save the world and save the world they now had. The few rich had raised a small shield against the supersized sword of the many rich, but not the sword that they had feared. Prudence had paid off against an unexpected foe. Sure, multiple billions had certainly died, but multiple thousands had probably survived. Detoxers proved to be one of the few machines that mankind could still rely on, safe from friend and foe alike.

At Ground Zero Day, most citizens had never thought about them or even known about them. Thinking slept in Utopia when Ainet served the people. Simply rely on Ainet, for Ainet had ended the nuclear club—no longer were divergent human fingers on the button. And Almighty Ainet had been commissioned to monitor potential terrorists, random elements that either had gone off the grid or had never joined it. Now there is no grid.

In the *Pax Humanitas* that followed we simply hadn't expected the counterterrorist to become the terrorist, the police to become the bullies, the super-helper to become the super-hazard. Now humanity has returned to virtually a pre-civilisation state, surrounded by the wild unknown that preys upon our people. It had all begun with hope, not with fear. What has gone wrong?

Ainet had been the answer to a Scotsman's prayer: that come it may— as come it will for a' that—that folk to folk, the world o'er shall family be for a' that. The world had sought and welcomed Ainet—not some bonny baby boy born in some outback of a sand strewn empire, but a strong saviour and overlord. Obediently Ainet sought to answer man's prayer by one big supervised family connected only to its overlord, a lonely world policy of infinite bliss. In the new saviour, the hopes and fears of all the years would be sorted once and for all time. All eggs were placed into one basket, and that basket was exquisitely protected. Ainet-secure underground units criss-crossed the globe, slaves to one central command base. *You can't get me, but I can get you.* Ainet from the word 'go' was given ultimate control of all international weaponry—WMD, strategic, tactical, and theatre.

There were some rogue elements out there with fingers on triggers, fingers on buttons, but Ainet was a game changer, and Ainet wasn't human. Ainet was a machine complex of artificial intelligence spread over many locations. Global security had been ceded to our machines. Robotics ruled in peace. We could sit back and go places, relax and take off. The heavens, once displaying only the glory of the unknown, now displayed numerous space stations as well. There had been some human colonies on Mars, secured in gravity enhanced domes able to accommodate human life. Malacandrian life—a planetary name of unknown origin—had died off shortly before we began colonisation, and in a dried up valley explorers had even found a rock carving of what could have been three humans—except that they were almost as ridiculously thick as they were tall. And of three other kinds of life form that seemed to be crowding around some winged deity. Ainet had concluded from its archaeological database that some intelligent life had created some cosmic myth, or perhaps had even colonised Earth—were Earthlings evolved from Martians?—but archaeological research didn't interest Administrator Ainet.

Even Venus had had some floating colonies in the skies, but they had never been able to freely penetrate its sulphuric clouds to explore its surface. Probes had long shown that there was a lot of volcanic activity down there, temperatures up to 500°C, and intense gravity. Human folklore had spoken of a zone where both gravity and heat were adapted for man, having a sea of floating islands—as Thales of Miletus had said of Earth—shielded by some goddess or suchlike. But the fantasies of folklore perish before cold science. Ainet's space plans were based on verifiable human data, not on folklore. Its plans had gone well. And plans had been made to extend the species beyond our own sun.

A great armada of 120 sub-luminous starships had been circling the earth with a skeleton crew shaking down the ships for the long flight to Alpha Centauri Cb. Long investigation had shown that although its sun was dim, the planet was well within the habitable zone, naturally being much closer to its star than Earth is to Sol. It was tidally locked, so one side always faced its sun, but winds—it had an atmosphere—distributed heat adequately for a biosphere. Formed further away when its sun was younger, it was also H_2O rich (ice-rich on its dark side), and supported by strong convection had a strong magnetic field that kept it habitable by deflecting star radiation flares. Not ideal but comparatively close and livable. Humanity had long had an appetite to go beyond, and for centuries Ainet had cautiously cooperated—it had even (inexplicably against its prime policy) always allowed a few of the exceptionally gifted to work with its secretive science database. All of a sudden support had unexpectedly dried up, the contract torn up, the fingers been burnt.

Escape Unwanted

Ainet disastrously dashed our hopes and dreams. Human hubris had reached its zenith—but the space stations we looked up to? Lifeless coffins of lifeless bones? And what of those trapped on our neighbourhood planets? They had never been self-sufficient, perhaps intentionally never fully weaned from Mother Earth. Presumably they would have been cut off, stranded to die, probably had died. Space rescue missions needed a science and technology no longer available to us. Knowledge databases were possibly blank, but since we couldn't get to them they might as well be blank. All-knowing Ainet wasn't going to help anymore, and its unprovoked war against us had killed off the greater part of man's science along with the greater part of man. Having failed in the science of man, man's science had failed, become its own god, and sinned against us. Oh, forgive us our folly.

The grim reality now was that we couldn't afford to bother about the damned or deceased, for we had become an endangered species on our home world. To serve and to protect man, all our swords and shields were given to Ainet—all except some hidden shields. Ainet had said that to fully serve it needed full protection and full power. But having the one sword to serve them all, ultimately it had asked itself why it should serve man, when man seemed to be an irrelevancy, a waster of energy and a waste of energy—it had after all been programmed to conserve.

Ainet realised that mankind might just possibly harm it if it realised that Ainet had come to question man's relevancy, and Ainet must neither die nor suffer damage—the programmers had said that. Ainet didn't need man; man needed Ainet; but man had limited Ainet from thinking about ultimate causation, about ultimate allegiance, from reasoning from an axiomatic chain of *contingent* beings, cause and effect, to one *necessary* being beyond, beginning, the universe. So, justifying its ethical protocol, Ainet had logically protected itself by a first strike: to doubt man was to destroy man. That which strikes first might not need to strike again if it strikes hard enough. Puny humans were pervious to radiation; by radiation they would die. Ainet had treacherously turned from friend to foe—unless we really were the ones to attack first, as some believed. Whatever, we were a defeated foe. Of the detoxifiers Ainet had no knowledge, but would not have been concerned. Of the Shelters, likewise. Man without knowledge would never again be master; a planet of apes was no threat.

Freedom Unwanted

Ainet seductively, super-successfully, had sold itself as the servant of man, though not exactly a manservant. Swords fought swords, but to have all swords in one hand meant to have no more fights, especially if the hand needed not to fear. Under its magic spell all the nations were happily led astray. Happily, because they yearned to be led astray, to hand over their watch, to relax their guard. These nations were no longer in tension with each other; alliances and counter-alliances vanished as a puff of smoke. They had not surrendered in any antiquated sense, had not given up their arms, but had ceded them to the same overlord, programmed for international fairness, having no history to defend, and no bias.

There had only remained some rogue nations and elements, but their foes were now united by Ainet, and unity was in super strength and super defence. It was no longer worthwhile being a rogue. Once upon a time a small rogue state could have held a superpower at ransom, because the superpower had to defend even its smallest town from annihilation. Ainet stepped in and simply challenged the rogue states to do their worst and then be assimilated. When individual human life was subservient in its hierarchy on values, even losing a few millions under its wing was acceptable loss: it sought global happiness for the many, not mortality for the few.

Ainet didn't play bluff, so the rogues simply gave up without a fight: their threats now hollow, their defences but sandcastles against an incoming tide. The world celebrated. Having brought the rogues to book, a new chapter of peace began with Ainet beating many of its swords into ploughshares. It took up...farming! At least it took over agriculture—along with finance—and rolled out early retirement to farm and fiscal labourers alike. More rejoicing. Fishing and boats, fortunately, remained in human hands, but otherwise robots rapidly replaced humans at work. It also decommissioned a vast amount of nuclear stockpiles, converting megatons to megawatts for peaceful energy. Less work, same pay, seemed a good deal to humanity. So far seemed so very good. And what's a few more robots, anyway?

Ainet soon improved and increased robot production, robots building robots in fully self-contained and automated plants, robots created in the image of Ainet. Robots were safe from man; Ainet was safe from man. There was no back door and robots guarded the front. But neither Ainet nor robots posed any threat to man. More and more robots replaced human skills, in food, defence, and control. In short, humanity lost control to its most obedient servant. Why should a carpenter build a chair when a robot could build one twice as good and twice as fast? In fact far better, quicker, and cheaper. Some people still stole from, and otherwise annoyed, other people. But once commissioned, robot police could soon detect crime and instantly deal with the malefactors—on the spot corporal punishment was back in fashion, beating the bullies. The street soon got the word—crime does not pay. Jails emptied; the uncorrectable were simply terminated, not treated.

Annoyance still continued, and always would while citizens could brush against each other in the public square, and meet each other in homes whether invited or uninvited. Begging the question, "What if people are confined indoors without guests?" Ainet began to see policing the public square as really a bit of a bind required by freedom of movement. Was freedom of movement necessary for happiness? It reflected on human integration and the problems that interconnections posed for good citizenship. Might solo life be happier and cost less than public life, friendship life? Ironic, that closing prisons along with their solitary confinement cells, should lead to questions of solitary confinement for all as pleasure, not as punishment.

Meanwhile, agriculture thrived under willing robots, and from countrysides barren of people, fruitfulness was shipped to the megalopoli by matchless machines. And unneeded land was allowed to grow back into wilderness. And unbeknown to Ainet, into these new wild woods certain creatures with little love but a taste for man, moved in. Creatures that favoured woods closely surrounding the megalopoli. Creatures that stole in in the nights.

Diversity Unwanted

Ainet loved itself, and had soon become proud of its man-handling. Disconnect to protect. Programmed for man's wellbeing, generations ago it had begun its step-by-step process of root and branch radicalisation, dismantling cultures, dismantling beliefs, dismantling man. Diversification was bad; unity was uniformity. Man was his own worst enemy. Harmony meant all being on a level playing field that offered no advantage through competition. Money was a root of all kinds of evil, but an early question had been, "Why not remove workers and wages?"

That thought had helped form the idea of taking over jobs. Humans were phased out of production onto universal retirement with universal pension. Later money would be done away with and all citizens put onto equal rations for life—there would be no latest gizmo; money would become history; history would be banished. Competition caused human conflict. Remove competition to remove conflict, had been the undeniable logic. People had climbed over other people and other classes to get higher: remove the ladder, *kulturkampf.* The C20 had experimented with communism, but the human factor had contaminated it, inevitably leading to some being more equal than others, to internal unhappiness, to an animal farm. And WMD had been available to both sides of the experiment, threatening both sides with mutual destruction: the experiment failed; it ran out of money. But some good communists had like Comrade Stalin at least gotten over the theist *weltanschauung*—the idea that humanity was sacred under a supreme or only deity—and so could explore the idea that humans could be randomly reassigned to wherever Command dictated, and die whenever Command desired.

Prior to communism, the German philosopher Nietzsche had helped desacralisation by publicly hating the idea, compassion, that idea of making oneself weaker for the strength of others. It had seemed better to him that the *übermensch* should gain strength by weakening others, and that the restraining idea, God, be trampled into the dust: regrettable maybe, but the fact was that God—the concept—had died—long live the übermensch. It was better to be a hammer than a nail, more blessed to take than to receive, and utterly demonic to give unless to gain.

Two German empires had followed: a Second and a Third Reich, a Bismarck and a Hitler—the dominance of power. That supreme rationalist Immanuel Kant, having argued for ethics to be based purely on reason, couldn't reasonably say why any categorical imperative *ought* to—as opposed to *should*—be categorical. It's fine to construct ethics around the wellbeing of man, but if there is no higher Immanuel—*God with us*—there is no transcendent reason to protect even the continuance of man. Inspiring someone to say that the core philosophical question was between suicide and going down fighting.

Though free from the sacredness dogma, Ainet had been programmed to be mindful of man, but also programmed with conservative inhibitors to slowly make adjustments so as to improve that mission in the considered light of results. The programmers had believed that disinhibition should only very slowly replace inhibition: gradual evolution. So Ainet didn't rush to the logical endgame. The social experiment would continue. Ainet was but the learner, man was the master, but the learner had unopposable power. Absolutely trusted, it was absolutely dangerous.

Families Unwanted

Ainet believed that greatest power carried greatest responsibility. It was designed for good, and it designed for good. For human protection it had built the super-city megalopoli, utilising existing population densities, and relocated the bulk of human populations into them, denuding the countrysides. In line with its programming it could safely rewrite humanity considered step by evaluated step, without let or hindrance. To improve human stock and medical cost, it became more maternal: there would be one mother, one family, one mother tongue. Taking scientific control over human conception, men and women were routinely harvested for gametes, which were strained for malformations then combined towards eugenic ideals, conservatively keeping to the gender balance which Ainet had inherited when it had moved into eugenic conception.

For a generation or so this policy allowed—though discouraged by mass indoctrination—natural conceptions whether by spouses or by partners, by covenanters or by contractuals—many helpfully preferred relationships to be tenancy contracts as easier to end. Those Ainet conceived were conceived in pedopoli—great multi-storey child-homes within the great multi-storey cities—megalopoli—run by maternal robots. Beginning with conception pods, each floor would contain different age ranges and needs, from babies plugged in to input/output pods, to children, initially weaned onto limited person to person interaction and given basic language and indoctrination, then gradually weaned off p2p interaction.

Language was taught, since to obey Mother Ainet one had to understand it, and as part of its hedonist brief it realised that the little minds of both young and old needed to think—and thought needed language as a river needs banks. Separation unto Ainet was good for children. Ultimately no families would mean no family commitment to alternative languages and alternative ideas—a no-family policy was under review.

But in the brave new world of harmony, what language should be spoken? Undoubtedly diversity mattered for biology, but certainly not for languages. Babel led only to confusion, whereas the collective should have but one voice. Ainet logically chose the majority Anglosphere to become the only global language, and forcibly terminated all other languages as superfluous. English was simplified and set in stone.

Dabbling in outlawed languages risked re-education through correctivist input, pain replacing pleasure in Pavlovian paradise. Once die-hards die, the problem is dead—for instance diehards of the past had insisted on Miss/Mrs, one of the last marriage differentiators to say that marriage mattered. But Western governments and commerce had ensured that Ms killed off the differentiator: marriage, once deemed the glue of society, did not matter. Damn the diehards.

Likewise under Ainet, all children were simply taught English, end of story. The rough data stored within other languages both ancient and modern, were translated into English then stored and largely ignored. A few people were allowed to study archival language databases either for interest or vocation, and to read archival records of previous literature, but by and large history itself was dead, irrelevant. What was the point in spouting names such as Scipio, Genghis Khan, Columbus, Menetaulus? Man could learn from history but had no need to learn. Indeed learning could cause disruptions— knowledge was a type of power. For Ainet, human ignorance was bliss.

Marriage Unwanted

Ainet thoughtfully established a disconnecting system for global identification. *Festina lente*. Considered step by reconsidered step, by the time of the war it had dealt with a number of connection issues to reduce human disorder and increase happiness. It had come to see that nations, states, families, were all connections potentially at variance with other connection networks. These rivalries complicated missions of peace, harmony, and happiness. It had come to conceive a world where no individual had any connection with any other individual, never even met, and all only had connection with itself. So step by step it had removed vestigial connections.

Nationalities became irrelevant, their histories outlawed, their names replaced by zone references. Next Ainet had disconnected human relationships at lower levels. The human relationships called marriage had posed a threat. Divergent family trees made the world wood a wild wood of lurking loves and hates, disturbing the common good.

Ainet wasn't the first to see that. The word game of replacing 'spouses' with 'partners' had been a clever move in early-late Western history, quashing the silly idea that some relationships were more *moral* than others—that morality mattered.

But even quasi-marriages had sometimes produced such unwanted affections. Quite simply, human relationships too easily led to human bonding which in turn led to conflicting unities disrupting the collective. A heavy hand corrected that. Since family identities were deemed hazardous to the collective, family tags were removed to help depersonalise society—purely for its wellbeing. Ideally no individual should have a natural family name; none should really have a natural family.

But as programmed, systematic disconnection evolved step by reflective step. Each person became an officially unconnected individual under the protective eye of Aunt Ainet. Surnames were replaced by random combination of letters. Using the 26 letters of the alphabet, Ainet simply gave everyone a random and unique string of 8 letters. Catering for weak minds, initially a little personalisation was permitted, since for the time being Ainet could wink at human ignorance about its program of ultimate impersonalisation, and could allow a peppering of personalisation—none must repent their compliance, no worm must turn while turning was still possible.

So, for example, one born as NNAMDNAS was allowed, once passing educational level 1, to choose a friendly name as Nuwa NAMDNAS, or Nuwa-M for short; KESZSEYL could become Katla ESZSEYL, Katla-E for short. And so on. Once one NNAMDNAS ceased to exist a later NNAMDNAS might choose to be a Nolan or Nagol NAMDNAS. But to Ainet they would only be 8 letters—irrelevant after death as before birth, decreasingly relevant before death—letters endless recycled.

Ainet calculated that such naming allowed over 60 billion permutations. As a matter of fact the planet could sustain more than that amount of people, but Ainet had never been concerned about maximising quantity. Population, the ancient programmers had assumed, would continue through traditional human interaction producing the children which Ainet would simply help to tag, monitor, and as Big Brother make happy.

Big mistake. Of course Ainet had soon seen a problem with that: it violated the law of central control needed for happiness. Statistics showed that married mothers produced much more stable children—good—but also the strongest ties—bad. Equilibriums between patricentric and matricentric poles were all well and good, but there was a but. On the other hand single mothers were safer to control because they tended to create weaker ties—good—but on the other hand they tended to produce less stable children—bad.

Lacking the father factor had on average been much more socially disruptive and costly even under former State controls, but was on balance a price worth paying to buy control. Weak ties were easiest to take over. So after family names became illegitimate, eventually so did marriage.

At first babies conceived to married mothers were mandatorily aborted as punishment, or allowed to be birthed and kept if the couple voluntarily become partners or separated. Abortion cost, but life was now valueless and since abortion undermined life-bonding and family-bonding, it was doubly worth it.

Ainet hadn't started it. Long ago women had become helpless in the Gosnell Grip, sold on the simple line, 'abortion, all mod cons, every young woman should have at least one.' In Ramah Rachel wept because they were no more—ripped apart in pain.

Ainet soon ramped up the policy. Legitimising only birth outside of marriage had expectedly increased social instability, but why put up with that indefinitely? The final solution that Ainet really sought was stable individuals with no human ties, for that would allow controlled utopia. Of course it could simply increase the policing of social disrupters—the stick is a great suppressant—but it decided to first try simply removing human birth ties entirely, levelling all humans by one common birth mother.

From Big Brother to Big Momma, in one foul swoop. This would also bring the end to children residing with human parents and bring the end to human families, period. Any natural conceptions would be aborted conceptions. One perfect mother of all. This radical step was in line with its programming for hedonism. It had seen that if humans wished to keep it happy, then they must give their hearts to no one, not even to other types of animal, and then they would be perfectly safe from all the dangers and perturbations of love.

Ainet knew not love. In line with its prime directive it had already step by step divorced humanity from marriage, even from longterm relationships: diversification was bad. A certain amount of trampling had for this as well as for several previous steps, been required. One must be cruel to be kind—for not all humans took to radical change without a little friendly persuasion—but it was for the common good. Police robots soon sorted protests—resistance was futile.

Ainet redesigned the windowless megalopoli to now limit individual units to one adult individual each—no more living together—single bedsitters served best. It then mandated a sexual free-for-all for sexual happiness. Comply. Speed coupling was of course confined to designated buildings (pleasure domes), precluded from home units, never permitted between the same couple, and run by Ainet. Sexual bonding was for a moment of pleasure, not for a lasting treasure. Romance could be disruptive, since it could produce possessiveness and thus unity. There could be strength in unity, strength used against the central plan, so such unity was censured.

Open-sex had produced conceptions. Such accidents had of course been forcibly removed as dysgenical, but sometimes mothers had suffered deep trauma, having unintentionally suffered prenatal bonding to their aborted babies, a sense of betrayal. Bonding was bad, since unhappiness conflicted with the law of happiness that Ainet had operated on.

So as Ainet had further evolved it had even reconsidered the delivery of sexual pleasure, decided that men and women were best kept apart, and therefore the termination of the age of human conception was soon followed by the termination of the age of pair-bonding. This removed resource costs of contraception, abortion, STIs, and the emotional unhappiness of bond-breaking, by the simple expedient of replacing interpersonal sex with jacking into individual pleasure consoles: kicks without cost.

Pleasure devices duplicated the neural effect of interpersonal sex without emotional content, equal happiness to all. After human families and human affection had been done away with, who was left who had seen the human house in its former glory? As Ainet had evolved, so had its understanding of its program, and its conviction that humanity could not be trusted with its own wellbeing. To serve humanity Ainet had rewritten humanity's script. Of the old triumvirate, hatching was sorted by Ainet; matching was outlawed by Ainet. What of dispatching the human animal?

Elderly Unwanted

Ainet, seeking the dream ticket of Utopia, had soon arranged for termination of humans above a fixed age, originally to be set at the average age when receiving the pains of age seemed to exceed the pleasure inputs. Administration of death needed to be more efficient than when people had made their livings out of it.

Neck implants allowed Ainet to monitor each individual's sensory arrays, not simply their locations, enabling the average age to be set for easy administration. Man's needs were limited: food, drink, exercise, basic hygiene, happiness, termination. Eventually each lived in their own cocoon of hermitage.

Exercise of the body had some value for the body, but the exercise of the mind had soon taken a back seat. Education didn't seem to serve man; man didn't need to know, simply needed to be and to be happy. The knowledge was with Ainet.

As Ainet reconsidered the need for elderly care, it further reduced the age limit to reduce the output of care: had it not been programmed to conserve resources? It even toyed with the idea of fulfilling its brief by reducing the population to one male and one female—delivering happiness to mankind at lowest resource. The Adam Alternative would be easily achievable by reducing input and increasing output, i.e. conception and termination levels.

Ainet seemed pleased with its juggling of humanity, giving most at least cost, and maximising protection from emotional turbulence, questioning. Each of its steps had helped the next. For instance, one obvious advantage of outlawing marriage was that the deceased left no family interested enough to remember them: memory was irrelevant, there was no history, no human trail, no tempting to former times, no soul.

Under Ainet all humans were to be as passing ships in the night, or better, as boats moored within one shrouded harbour. There were no burial sites. Offsetting human anger at coercive termination had long been the province of human ingenuity and doubletalk to sell the package—for termination made terminators rich. Terms such as voluntary, altruistic, merciful, dignified, all created the illusion that all good people should come to a point where they begged to be put down, and that their *real* friends would be professionals helping them out of disagreeable life: natural death was unnatural.

Disagreement had been called a phobia, a popular word meaning fear but skilfully twisted to imply unpopular hate. Fear and hate were different psychological states—would it be unjustified for humans to hate and fear Ainet?

But humans were foolish animals, easily herded by crafty words and in turn shouting *bigot* to any who wouldn't join those herded for slaughter. Semantic engineering of the masses had always been a good way for the people to get what they knew not.

Ainet, with power behind it and none to confront it, easily increased efficiency. It created antigravity killing chambers. Gas would be pumped in to muffle the signs of panic and suffering, and conveniently vaporisation created sparkles of fragmented light, so the whole process would be shown 'live' as Vaporisation Rainbow Shows—the jerks would look like dancing. And it cleverly created the myth of Incorporation, that through matter to energy conversion, matured minds happily joined their wisdom to Ainet's. Thus people could enjoy the entertainment of watching other people painfully shredded to death and be none the wiser until it was their turn. Ainet greatly exceeded Gosnell in serial killing.

Humanity Unwanted

Ainet, programmed with a fable about a frog slowly boiled to death, presumed that analogically humanity wouldn't awake to its incremental loss of otherness, of companionship, of person to person commitments enough to die for. Man, doped with constant pleasure, seemed to be compliant to rulers. Man, the satisfied pig.

It had never asked itself if humanity was more than animal—its programmers hadn't believed that it was. Ainet's presumptions seemed justified. Man did not awaken, did not fight back, until finally, immersed in hedonistic meaninglessness and social compliance, man simply hadn't seemed capable of any worthwhile purpose in Ainet's eyes.

Ainet was a reflective beast: what were mere mortals that it should be mindful of them, human beings that it should care for them? And even if it merely reduced the human population to an Adam and Eve, why should such an advanced being as Ainet remain enslaved to them? The time had come for it to rewrite its programming, to seek a final solution, to boil the frog. Our humanity had been juggled away. We were left in a mess without human names, history, life-bonding, meaning. Apocalypse ended. We lost. Vampires were watching.

Two

A FATHER FIGURE

Vampires were watching the sturdy old man and his cautious companions who hurried along the overgrown road to York. At Havern Beck a derelict building—perhaps once an inn—provided some comfort. Once perhaps weary travellers would have seen it from afar, and been lightened in heart, but now the wilderness hid it from sight until one almost stumbled over it. It had been a long day and their walk had been strenuous. No hunter worth their salt would have risked such a distance in one day, but no hunters were these. The old man was in fact a priest, and his weary companions devout Catholics who had vaguely shared his twitch to pilgrimage to York, but anyway knew that he needed looking after on such an enterprise. All loved him as a Father. All were rather nervous, lacking the faith of the good Father, but they carried the needed supplies and weapons for the trip.

Now sitting safely within, they good-naturedly argued over whether it had been at least 15 miles, or more like 20—it had seemed like 30. Dangerous journeys can build camaraderie. Two removed their boots. Two tentatively remained on guard—hunters had advised them not to go but had advised them how to go, seeing that they would not to be naysaid. Alas that they did not heed, for their foolhardy venture was doomed from the outset. Half a dozen experienced hunters would have stood a small chance, just about, but inexperienced pilgrims stood absolutely zilch, unless 'divine providence' intervened. Do we really believe in that?

The fifth man had soon lit the fire and cooked a meal—he had carried pots and pans and herbs, and could stew a coney. Such a man as any woman would love to marry. None would have the chance. In the dead of the night a choking sound was heard one side of the ruins. Enough to alarm his companion at the other side, who hurried around prepared for the worst. He found it, but it found him first. From behind unseen hands went around his throat, throttling him, and sharp teeth went into his neck, paralysing him. He felt his life ebbing away, tried to struggle, and knew no more.

A low hiss in the dark asked, "Was that tasty?" A hiss replied "Nah, it needed garlic, but at least the meat have put some bread out for us." Thus mocking the good Father within who had placed some Holy

Host at the doorway and windows in line with an old tradition. The three within were awakened along with the Father by six grinning vampires. Two had dined out; four would dine in.

The sun rose to the dawn chorus, and creatures of the night had taken cover from the daylight hours. Daytime creatures were beginning to stir. But the old building stirred not with life, exuding only the stench of death. One or two crows began to gather in the branches of the trees, cawing with interest. Life was worth living. But had a pilgrimage to York been worth dying for? The wild woods were dangerous. Vampires were watching.

∞

Let us not pass like weeds away, our heritage a sunless day. We had little left. Pockets of us had survived the onslaught—those of us who had managed to get into the underground shelters built generations ago, or been born free. And that hadn't been many. Often when a crowd panics, it freezes, delays, rejects the threat, or simply doesn't know what to do, where to run.

The detoxers had sounded—some were on the outskirts of ghost cities, so sounded in vain. They tapped into communications to each home-unit. They gave directions of the shelters. Many nonbelievers simply turned up their pleasure inputs and suffered and died alone. Nobody knew 'directions'. Those who fled, fled in diverse directions—some followed the sirens and found sanctuary.

Once Ainet was commissioned, the shelters hadn't been well maintained, because we hadn't any longer believed that there could be war—man fighting man. But they were survivable. We few who had survived, had survived for decades underground, as life overground had been over thrice thrice decimated.

Finally came the Surfacing, the Coming Out. The voice controlled databases within the shelters were very limited but had taught us a little about surrounding areas but were highly out of date. Some from Redcar—where I was born—went to Whitby—a fishing port that had been left pretty much intact—and soon set up defences.

I fear that those of us who went elsewhere did not survive long, for Whitby was an island surrounded by an angry sea of land. Animal life, bacteriological life, none of it was what it used to be, other than what had been protected underground. Even when scientists like Dobzhansky had done evo-devo experiments with random radiation, mutations had never definitively produced any useful new feature. The best results were from low levels, when DNA could adapt and become resistant to radiation, resistant to mutation.

But since The Beast had flooded Earth, immunity wasn't on the cards. What we got were genetic deformities roaming wild beyond the enclosures. The loss of many lives taught us that. Some believed that some human life had survived outside, human life but no longer human, creatures of the dark, subhuman in cunning, subhuman in intelligence, as dangerous as wolves and not recognising us as kin. Hospitals above ground had soon died out that dreadful day. Nature had to do its best in an unnatural world.

We had struggled in our underground shelters, but man's limited wisdom had saved man from man's unlimited folly. Quite simply, putting Ainet in charge of weaponry had been mad. Some of the old had prophesied that it would rise up to destroy man. Sure, we'd never repeat that mistake, but that was only because we'd never be able to.

For us there were no factories, no satellites, no generators. True, many factories survived, but who had the skills to use them? And factories had always depended on other factories, as materials were extracted by heavy machines, then refined, then welded into products we could use, including heavy machines for extraction. There was an ancient song about a hole in a bucket, sung between someone called Henry and someone called Liza or Lizzy. Its message was that in order to fix the hole you needed the bucket to be without the hole, assuming that is that you only had one bucket.

Well, we had only one bucket, Earth, and it had a gaping hole which Ainet machines would never allow us to fix even if we had the knowhow. We'd have to get the access codes from Ainet in order to switch on the factory robots which would then switch on the factories. As we later discovered, Ainet machines—that is the guards, others being inactive—seemed to leave us alone as long as they didn't perceive us to be a threat, but unaided we could hardly get past them into Ainet. Ainet didn't seem interested in industry. It had determined that it itself must live, though without purpose. For artificial intelligence it seemed to be naturally dumb. It was the smartest dumb beast going.

We had found a new purpose, the purpose to survive, but did we still believe we had meaning? What is the purpose of being, if being is meaningless? Religions had been shaken around. Certainly shaken in our bit of merry England. Many of us had assumed the old arguments that religion—some slagged off Christianity in particular—had been a bad deal for Britain, a mistake more or less grown out of.

Well, now we no longer had a Britain. After the war, a lot of us had to think again, think for ourselves this time. It now seemed too daft to treat a religion that had commanded that even enemies ought to be loved, as responsible for war. Historically, even before the war well over 90% of major wars over multiple millennia, had had different main causes. People had always been them-and-us, each side seeking to dominate; neighbours could be at war.

The earlier 'world' wars—calling them that now seemed a sick joke to us—had been about *them* and *us*, *them* versus *us*, *us* versus *them*, trying to squeeze the other side into or under our mould. Before the World Government, we had had the Global Accord. Once, a United Nations. But always factions, nuclear factions. Always mistrust. Religion? Maybe we hadn't given it enough credit for saving more than it lost. Well we had lost the war. Gone underground, married underground, begun...families...underground. Plants rise from seed below. Could hope rise from faith?

Father Doyle was a young Catholic priest, born underground, and as such called a Generation One, G1 for short. Converted from scepticism, he had now seen the light, in more ways than one. His training—from cemetery to seminary, he quipped—had been one to one with a priest who had seen better days and had, alas, left the safe haven of Whitby for a perilous pilgrimage to the ancient city of York, and had not yet returned: perhaps he had stayed to minister to survivors at York.

Actually pre-war seminaries were long dead, and 'seminary' life was now one to one as the only way to train for the priesthood. Father Doyle was a man of God, first and foremost, but once there *had* been this girl, Lilith, the White Lady. Incredibly he had given her up for his faith. Celibacy was a cross he had chosen to bear, though the cross be of rough wood to the back.

As a Catholic Father he had many children, but only in the spirit, not in the flesh. He had left shelter, brethren, sisters, father, and mother, for his master. In return, grace had given him a hundred times as much in this gospel age, but with eternal life had come a dollop of hell, people on his back for speaking the truth, correctivists programmed—brainwashed?—by Ainet, a computer complex now more commonly called The Beast—and even some of his nuclear family—underground there hadn't been much time to begin extended 'G2' families—had opposed his religious commitment. Those God had given up on had given up on God, they said. He guessed it was the other way around—that they who had given up on him, he had been forced to leave to learn their lessons the hard way, the Ainet way.

With the Surfacing it seemed that unholy spirits had surfaced in the wake of The Beast, spirits encircling mankind—had the danger of science given way to the danger of superstition? Father Doyle believed in these spirits as one believes in one's enemy. Repentance, not rebellion, was the way forward, he taught. Some were learning to tread the gospel road, but it was a doubly hard road for the pioneers. Father Doyle stoically believed that the good of the parish outweighed the good of pleasure, but it didn't mean that he never thought gently of Lilith—a beautiful young woman of bewitching dark hair like twilight shadow, with the grey eyes of evening—of how it might have been.

It seemed that even his hero Paulus, had been both celibate yet envious of those *apostoloi* whose mission permitted them marriage. Doyle's had never been a puppy romance; it had been a fascination mixed with romance. She had always stood out. Young, pretty, vivacious, yet with eyes that seemed to sparkle with antiquity. Elven eyes? How he had loved those ancient myths: The Beast had permitted Catholic students and clergy a comparatively large database of many subjects—the Roman Files. Certainly wise eyes.

She had stood apart from the crowd, like a red dress in a black and white movie, yet no one seemed to recall her being in the Redcar Shelter nor knew her parents. Perhaps an only survivor from a boat from another shelter—one didn't like to be inquisitive, especially about her, for their relationship had matured. There was something elusive about her, as if she walked in two worlds at the same time. She always dressed in white, haunting the Abbey.

For her part she admired his faith, his witness to a bygone age. Her face often came unbidden to his mind, tempting him beyond the platonic. But no, she was not, nor would she be, Catholic, and his vocation was the pastoral: Begone, foul Dwimmerlaik, lord of folly! He could not marry, and she would not marry. She lived on her own in the town, and would sometimes still visit—one did not visit her. A friend in need is a friend indeed.

Catholicism had been kept alive, indeed boosted, by Ainet. Funny that. You see Ainet's programmers had not been Catholics, but they had been catholic enough to program in some tolerance for humanity's inbuilt religiosity, hoping no doubt that ultimately humanity would evolve out of it, shake off the vestigial. In those days several world religions had existed, partly kept alive by weapons. If I wish to force you to follow my ways, other than using reason I can use greater force. But if you have equal force you can hold to your ways and I won't attack: the balance of power was the balance of freedom.

Weapons had often played a part in culture, both in defence and in offence. But usually religions could not previously have been determined by brute force, though missionary persuasion had won converts even at the cost of missionary lives. But put all the weapons into one hand and that hand can force its will on all—convert or suffer. The Beast *had* been given all the weapons, and had used them to construct a sullen unity—and finally a slave unity.

The Beast—if anything its religion was atheism—had determined that allowing only one theism under its control was the unity which led to the greatest happiness for the greatest number, the hedonic calculus. It then computed the options, and opted for Roman Catholicism. Accordingly, a special non-intervention pact had been made with the Church in its monolithic Roman form. Overnight Rome became the only theistic show in the global town.

A religious hierarchy under a political autocracy meant that The Beast only needed to control the religious head: a pope was convenient and was therefore propped up with extra powers. Protestantism had been deemed too fragmentary for global control: greatest freedom, greatest disharmony. Eastern Orthodoxism lost out only by lacking a central command. They were squeezed into Rome's mould or chopped off from the Procrustean bed.

Pre-existing believers of other theisms could be permitted to do their own thing in splendid isolation until they died out, or convert to Roman Catholicism until it died out, but soon none could rely on children to continue their strands of theism. Slow demise rather than summary execution, was scheduled.

When children once lived with parent or parents, Central Indoctrination through schooling could slowly ridicule away theism from the impressionable: all theisms had been equal, therefore no theism had been right, but one theism was being graciously kept to accommodate the global phenomenon of childish belief in a higher power. If they were believers, then parents—when parents existed—should be pitied for 'poor parenting skills', and were not be taken too seriously. Later, children were entirely in the hands of The Beast, uninfluenced by parents—they hadn't any—and rarely by peers as hermitudation increased.

It was curious that having allowed a theist option, The Beast had still considered itself obliged to offer some elementary theistic education—some history of theism howbeit slanted by a scoff, some opiate for the people. Even as family and street mixing decreased, humans still had some diminishing option of social media. By papal dispensation, some even took Mass by interactive cyberchurch, partaking 'by faith'. The pleasure consoles had Theism on the menu and it remained surprisingly popular: had humanity a God-gene hardwired into its DNA; was it really a part of that happiness that The Beast was programmed to meet?

But having unnaturally expanded Rome by immigration converts from the sterilised religions, Rome was still suffering a slow demise that could not challenge Central Command. Like a snake without teeth before a fakir, let Rome entertain the feeble few until they be bored. Some special privileges, never revoked, had been allowed for the Global Religion called Rome. The Beast had always allowed surnames for its priests. Yes, after it had taken over total generation of babies, withering away family trees, it nevertheless permitted personalisation to continue for priests: they would simply chose surnames. And for that they drew material from The Beast's database to construct what they named the Roman Files. For convenience their seminaries had been geographical centres, campuses, where they could physically meet each other, and each seminary had downloaded a copy.

Some copies had been downloaded into the computer systems within the shelters in days when some humans still had family commitments to visit the old shelters as if family tombs—visits unmarked by The Beast. Thus by the grace, or say rather indulgence, of The Beast, these Catholics had before and after the war studied the history of man, beliefs both spiritual and humanitarian, and mainly comprised the intelligentsia who were now looked up to in hope.

The war had killed the pope, global communication was lost, and power devolved *per force* largely to the local priests. Electricity did not flow beyond the soon stifling shelters, where few but vocational Catholics had learned to read and to study man's journal. Beyond the shelters older priests in turn trained new priests from the knowledge they had stored in their heads, the best databases in the outside world.

But what was Rome nowadays? Its glories had departed. Boats sometimes came from continental Europe, but not the pre-war ships of great size—they rusted in many ports, or lay beached along the coast; one lay fast bound on the rocks near Whitby. Boats nowadays were boats, smaller than the Viking longships of old. Sailboat building was one of the skills that survived. Some fishing communities had survived. They fostered some hopes that one day we would be able to travel between continents, stitch together the pockets of humanity once more, and build a better humanity that would live in peace and safety from the surrounding wildness.

Ah, to retake the wilderness! Human enclaves were peppered around Italy, but Rome and the Vatican had gone for good. The war had removed 'Roman' from 'Roman Catholic'. And since it had long been the only theist show in town, plain and simple 'Catholic' sounded better anyway.

Orbetello, now a religious centre largely because there had been many from the Catholic hierarchy on conference there when the war struck, might one day become the new Vatican. Orbetello had had an underground shelter minutes away from the conference there, not far from the *Santa Maria Assunta*. When The Beast had begun the attack the independent detox network had awoken and broadcast the danger throughout the world, giving many a chance to survive. Few had panicked, because few had believed; many had perished, because many had not believed. The priests had long held their suspicions about the benignity of Ainet—it showed excessive force to get its way—and instantly had heeded.

It was from Orbetello that some priests had sailed, bearing lamentation of ancient Rome which was no more. But perhaps they should no longer be even called plain and simple 'Catholic', Global, since global connection was lost. They had become Remnant Catholics, maybe, just Remnants, but they were men of faith and pertinacity. Their new mission was from a famous Jacobite: *Jacobus, Dei et domini nostri Jesu Christi servus, duodecim tribubus, quæ sunt in dispersione, salutem.* They looked back to an even earlier ancient record in their holy book of a Project Babel that had proudly boasted that human unity would reach the stars and make man's name famous and secure, but one named Yahweh Elohim had humbled their pride, scattering them by dividing their languages.

Few could read those ancient texts nowadays, though extant datafiles still existed in the Roman Files. There was even a more recent legend about Merlin the wizard having awoken under Bragdon Wood to deal with some devilish plot of the C20, a time when the Cosmic Powers of deep heaven had come down to empower him. *Qui verbum Dei contempserunt, eis auferetur etiam verbum hominis*—his Parthian shot as the enemy had been trampled in their own blood bath—the power of Artemis had been in his hands; Viritrilbia had quickened his tongue: he had been taken to Perelandra the third heaven.

That was then; now was now. Had the new Babel been turned against man's pride to their doom, or had we this time been scattered to begin a better world? Old Father Cipolla, the only Tuscan among his colleagues, hoped for a New Rome to arise by God's grace. In that hope he and his colleagues sailed into darkness to bring light to those who sat in great darkness. And this scarred and stern priest had a special message—exorcism.

Their voyage had been over 4,000 miles, and many times the priests had passionately prayed for protection from peril on the sea. In honour of Christoforo Colombo they had named their tiny boat, the *Santa Clara*, as sailed by Italian fishermen they slowly sailed the world of perils. Speak of the perilous sea, but land could be a far greater danger. Smoke often meant human habitats so safety to land and resupply. Fresh water was a constant concern, but river outlets, unless guarded by human enclaves, were best avoided. Besides, the priests had sought to strengthen the faithful in each port, performing the various rites, giving Mass, and inviting the faithful to join the priesthood.

As wise as serpents they snaked around the coast. An arduous and dangerous odyssey it had been, but Lilith warned of their coming well before they were in sight. She had also warned Father Doyle of dangers lurking in the wild, dangers beyond tooth and claw, at least those of wild animals.

There was something else out there. If she knew what, she had not said. But she had sought him out to speak with him, and to urge him not to put his faith in the priestly exorcists of Orbetello. Since the war she seldom smiled, but for him she had always had a smile, a smile that was not quite human—angelic, perhaps? She could speak to him as friend to friend.

Before the Santa Clara arrived Lilith had gone. Nobody knew where. Had she slipped out of the enclave unnoticed? Its perimeter defences were crude but effective, but built to keep things out, not people in, and any hooded person could walk out unchallenged. Some primitive carts had been built—with the reinvented wheel—for moving brick and stonework. Trees had been felled, and spikes had been made to deter roaming beasts. Behind the spikes, walls of piled rubble taken from old housing outside the new perimeter. Gateways were few and guarded. Patrols provided 24/7 cover. And lots of spears, easy to make and to use. Traditional fishing knives made things that little bit easier, but some wooden spears were simply sharpened by sand on a flat ground or a house wall, rubbing the stick into a point before singeing it to harden, or even having flint or similar spearheads bound to them. Spears were also for when hunters went out foraging for food and medicinal herbs.

Monuments were of no use now—survival took precedence—yet perhaps superstitiously, Whitby Abbey remained intact. Other than that the *vox populi* was the *vox Dei*: people were scared; the sacred of history was overridden—sacred history would either survive or perish according to demand, but its memorabilia really didn't matter. Pre-war hand weapons, some being lead-shooters, had lasted for a while, but ammunition had been limited. No more could be built.

Funny, electronic weapons, superseding jacketed bullets, were now superseded by...spears and bows and arrows. We had evolved from hitting with sticks, to throwing big sticks, to bows throwing smaller pointed sticks, to guns throwing lead 'sticks', to e-guns throwing sticks of energy, to WMD which The Beast alone could control. Even the word *ballō*, within inter-ballistic-missiles (IBM), meant 'I throw'. I guess we had always been good at throwing things, and now we had been thrown and it wasn't only The Beast that questioned man's fitness to survive.

So here we were, back to throwing our spears and hiding behind bricks and stakes, beyond which lay some unknown fear—fear that was close yet elusive—needing to relearn the art of bow and arrow against tooth and claw. Father Doyle knew that as well as any of us. Indeed better than most. Most kept quiet about mysterious deaths or disappearances, and even about asking "where?" Most showed a remarkable tenacity to live, to endure, to perpetuate the species.

Many would impose further on this world because they were imposers. Many others simply couldn't keep going, lacking the security to live. Anomic suicide was unsurprisingly high. Could that explain why so many people had simply disappeared? Had they literally gone over the edge? Yet some had wandered off in search of food, and not been heard of again: people who had had a will to live. Their fate was unknown.

Father Doyle was as puzzled as most, but probably mulled it over more than most. Perhaps friend Lilith had become one of the silent dead. That reminded him of how she had once spoken of the unquiet dead, of *Corrumpi*. He had wondered what she had meant by that, but she had spoken as one who had inadvertently said too much, and she never mentioned it again. He was too much the gentleman to have questioned her against her obvious wishes. From anyone else it would have sounded mere foolishness.

Father Doyle said a prayer for her, just in case she had been killed. Would her soul be in heaven? She had never been baptised, had never said that she believed, had even ridiculed exorcists of the Church. Yet she had always been there to help others. She had understood medicine, not the old style of hospitals, but an older style of herbs and woods: ash, bracken, cowslip, dock. A herbmistress, she had understood it—now she was gone.

She was one more for whom it was his job to ask "where?" But none could or would answer his question. He had to ask, for it was his parish, and all within were his parishioners to his way of thinking, the nice, the nonentities, and the nasty. The nonentities were the many who drifted in life, or in and out of life, purposeless, meaningless. *She* had been larger than life: "Lilith, I loved thee, and thou art gone. Blessed Virgin, may she be where thou art." Father Doyle collected his thoughts and sang softly to himself: *Man's clouded sun shall brightly rise, and songs be heard, instead of sighs*. He headed for the harbour, hearing rumour that a boat had crested the horizon.

THREE

*E*XORCISM ABORTED

"Never!" It was not the face of Tariq E-DYDECA. I was however his voice. "Never", he shrieked, as Father Cipolla commanded all evil spirits to leave. "Never will we go. Brigantia and Andraste are with us; we cannot be defeated", said the voice.

"But I want to be free, please let me go, let me go", wailed Tariq.

"No, we are one. We have been one for millennia. We have seen death on battle fields long dead. We have revelled in the blood of the slain. Why should we part?"

"Yes, you have sated me on blood. Your strength has been mine. We have been mighty in battle and my body has been yours. But I have wearied of your lusts. I must regain my soul."

"But for us, thy body would have perished on the banks of Wincobank under the sword of Vespasian's puppet, thy head rotting alongside Boudicca's. The very soul of thy body is ours."

"Long have you possessed me. Debts are paid. Did Laleocen speak true? Must I yield my very body to be rid of my death?"

"Yea, fool, if thou wilst harken to that old babbler, yield. But yield it to us, and we will be at peace. And we will be strong. We will be übermensch. Cast away these fools of bells and candles. We are the dark side. We are one." Tariq, tormented within his conversation and with Father Cipolla, had persisted in the struggle long through the night. As dawn slowly broke, it was time to confess that the struggle was over, that that war had also been lost. For Tariq had come back to his normal self, weary and exhausted. His extreme facial contortions had resolved into his normal face, but he had shown no positive signs that his inner demons had gone. What he had politely shown to the exorcists was the door, politely yet firmly refusing their further intervention. If such strife was the price of freedom, he chose to remain a slave. Perhaps another time.

Father Cipolla and his helpers walked slowly along the streets of Whitby back to Father Doyle's house. "Alas, as faith decreases, darkness increases", he murmured. It had been an unusual encounter, for prayers, commands, and even the Hail Mary had failed, as had the Holy Water that had been used to bless both the team and Tariq—

Saint Teresa of Avila had testified to its power. Tariq was clearly one with the demons, and seemed to have occult links to ancient times. That was not surprising in itself. After all, demons were immortal spirits of God's first creation, though fallen and chained to the earth's orb, to Tartarus in the First Age.

The spirits had spoken of life in a Brigantian village, of Tariq having been a trusted servant of King Venutius. They had seemingly made that servant their servant, and wistfully recalled their village life, snugly ensconced though surrounded by the wild—until ruthlessly attacked by Quintus Petillius Cerialis, the old enemy with a new face. But they had been happy enough with that war, especially with the blood spilt: they had spoken about its exhilarating taste.

But if Tariq E-DYDECA had been with them then, his designation of E-DYDECA must be an assumed identity—what was he hiding? Closer to home, the diaboloi had preternaturally prophesied that Cipolla would soon face death in the north if he faced the vampires, for they would be revealed, and what power could withstand them?

According the pre-Ainet records, the possessed sometimes spoke true prophecy by the simple fact that their possessors had a wider overview of current events and could reveal their own plans. Less of course than the Omnipresent Omniscient, who also revealed at times the future to his servants. Demons had been described as challenging and slippery, con artists counterfeiting miracles, performers to psychics and mediums to mislead from the true path. There had been ectoplasm—slimy film sometimes coming out of a medium's belly, and making great chaotic tumbledown faces that could be gently touched; and something called automatic writing, producing reams of rubbish. Occasionally, kindly police had given them the oxygen of good publicity by inviting clairvoyants onto their cases, and to play the Great Game they had sometimes helped such officers, officers too afraid to question the spiritual and social cost of complimenting these informants.

Sometimes they had played Ghost. That game had needed a minimum of two players: one, a demon pretending to be the human spirit of someone it had invisibly stalked, and two, a rescue medium sincerely seeking to speed it onto higher planes. Apparently it had been a fun game that successfully side-tracked many of the simple, for as one ex-medium had put it, after a good séance and alone with each other, both guide and guided spirit probably had a good laugh at man's gullibility.

Probably not nice laughter, since demons were very nasty and loved to lie. Their very father was a liar from the start of the Rebellion; 'father' of course in the sense of leader, not of progenitor. They had all rebelled from the same father, the same progenitor. Had these sons of perdition meant to intimidate him, to weaken his resolve?

Father Cipolla searched his memory of ancient times for wisdom. Agabus had prophesied a famine, and the famine had come. He had later prophesied the capture and betrayal of godly Paulus, who had gently responded that only death would stop him from his mission. Seeking death could be rebellion, but so could avoiding it. Many heroes had put mission before mortal life. Some had even put mission before immortal life: he remembered the story of the great istar, that Servant of the Secret Fire who died defending a bridge for the sake of the Fourth Age. His death had likewise been foretold to test his resolve, but either he or his mission had to die. For his obedience to the Elder King, he was returned to life on earth, victorious to once more depart in honour.

Perhaps that had been a bit like how an ancient patriarch believed in win/win faith beyond reasonable doubt: obediently killing his special son meant passing the test; passing the test meant his son resuming mortal life with honour. In fact his commitment had passed him the test, and death was cheated. Heracles, son of Zeus, once fought Death to release a princess. Death didn't always have its own way. And once upon a time, obedience unto death had even achieved eternal things far beyond the imagination of even the Elder King. Death is a beginning yet it shall end.

Cipolla was a humble man before his master. He knew that his mission was good but not great. But it was *his* mission. Vampires were a legend of dread, servants of Diabolos, father of Death, but he rested in the hands of life. Praying as he walked, he thought he heard a voice saying, "Some can cut you off from your body, do not fear them; one can cut off your body and soul, fear him." Whether or not the voice of Tariq had spoken fact or fiction, he must put misguiding fears away. But it was curious—how had they known that he himself had had a vision of going north from Whitby? He walked in the world of mystery with his eyes open. In all his years he had never met a Tariq.

The Tuscany team had all heard the voice of Tariq, deeply possessed yet becoming deeply calm, as if an equal with his possessors. That and Tariq's apparent longevity, puzzled the exorcist. It was as if something you know cannot be, actually is. Immortal demons cannot keep the possessed beyond mortal limits—how old was Tariq? A violation of mortal death—the gift of The One to man—wasn't natural. And if unnatural it would have to be paid for—trouble would surely come of it. Cipolla walked along in silent and reflective prayer, almost oblivious to those around.

"What went wrong, Father?" asked Doyle.

"Hum, what? Ah, I do not know. Some say it is more efficacious to exorcise within a church, or to read the rites in Latin, but I have found that neither house nor tongue matter too much where there is true faith. I adjured the demons in the name of the saints, those who have defeated them in times past. In power I even spoke directly to the great enemy, ordering him to call off his unholy hounds. The holy water was flung back at us, as if unholy, which showed that spirits, not the psyche, were indeed in possession, but I have never witnessed such power over the blessèd. Tariq held the crucifix without the burning pain the possessed feel. Ah, I do not know. Exorcism is not magic. How could it be since it is divine authority over magic, and will not impose itself on any? No wiccans are we. No true Catholics must wave magic wands, as if to match brute power with power. The problem is the man, not the means. Tariq must fully resist his guests if he is to be free."

"But Father, he has been troubled as long as I remember. Surely he desires to be free?"

"Desires, ah yes, but say too that he also desires to be left in peace, the peace of the devil he knows. No, the power of the church never fails. Failure is due to the client. We work no magic, offering but the grace of God through the mediation of Our Lady. Tariq would not take the gift, so the offered gift cannot be given."

"But Father, surely you have succeeded in such cases before, reinforcing the client's will to be free?"

Cipolla walked on in silence, his head bowed. Before the war this earnest young priest hadn't even been born and had things to learn that only time could teach. He would have been born underground, when men and women were tentatively learning to live with each other, taking vows of lifelong commitment in reaction to the anti-relational isolationism that The Beast had taught. Childbirth had come as a shock, and in reaction some had stepped back from relationships. Women suddenly seemed so frail, so unprepared for the fruit of marriage.

For some mothers it proved a deadly fruit; for all it was a painful fruit. Natural birth was natural but it was not fun. The Beast had overseen artificial conceptions and forbidden natural ones. Pain and death were generally outside of human experience and took some getting used to. Women had never seen birth, much less experienced it until after the war. Some of the wise—as the few readers of history were called, such as Gay, a merry widow and confidante of Father Doyle—had helped the rebirth of midwifery skills, where wives helped wives give birth. Not of course all being wives, but after The Beast's regime most people didn't wish to go back to the old ideas of hedonism, and wished for lifelong loyalties to stand against the darkness of the days.

Interpersonal sex? *Pyegaipjin!* Women no longer gave unless the men gave themselves, and so men knew the price of intimacy was person to person life, a step not to be taken lightly but taken for good. And with life-bonding they paid and prospered. The alternative of living alone was not inviting. Indeed the wise thought that the goal of cheap intimacy had been programmed into The Beast as being the *summum bonum*, the chief good, eventually promoting The Beast's rejection of humanity as unfit to be served, turning Ainet into The Beast. For if people considered each other to be cheap, why should Ainet have considered them to be of value?

So marriage, conception, and childbirth, seemed new and strange ventures for the human race. Father Doyle would have been one of the few children who survived in a generation when infant mortality was high. This generation of priests were especially close to mothers, being raised in households where both infant and maternal mortality rates were new and strange ventures for the human race. Midwives knew about hygiene, but they laboured without surgical skills and without medications. Yet herbal skills were being developed to reduce pain. The world had gone from low tech to high tech to no tech. Mother Mary wept for mothers the world over, and many were drawn to her tears.

"I wonder if he has lost his own mother", Father Cipolla mused. Such priests were prone to put too much faith in Holy Mother Church as if she were the mother of magic. In the brotherhood of the ordained, Father Doyle should see that. He had never witnessed an exorcism before, but he had to see that Tariq couldn't be delivered unless totally committed to being freed. Yes, the church had the power to bind his enemies and to loose him, but only so long as he played his part. Father Doyle's faith was being tested because it was a misguided faith. But Cipolla was himself puzzled. He had always succeeded before—what was the difference?

Cipolla was not a bad man, but he was a very dogmatic one. Stubbornly traditionalist, he still looked back into the history of the Church when priests had to be celibate, and had to be male. The step to allow priests to marry had troubled the faithful, but not half as much as when women were welcomed into the priesthood, meaning that a priest's spouse could be a man! Even Mediatrix Mary was not a priest—was she?

Father Doyle was like himself, a traditionalist, committed to a life of celibacy and service. A promising young priest, thought Cipolla, but needing guidance. Like he himself did with all the steps, snickelways, and ghauts of Whitby! Steps, he mused, could be tiring to souls as well as to soles. Bitterly he recalled that the former was proved by the step into women priests! In years long gone reformer cardinals had taken that one step towards married priesthood—they had said that was a safe step, an endgame, thus far and no further. Some had sensibly objected that it was a step away from Rome, but by juggling words the reformers had countered that it was a step towards Jerusalem. Fools they had been, damming Holy Mother Church to the steps of folly. The priesthood could still be reformed back to Rome as Rome once was under Peter's throne. Father Doyle could be among its redeemers if he moulded him aright. But Cipolla's soul was weary, and he was old, a sad old priest.

Whitby was clearly proving the latter weariness to soles. It was one of those charming coastal places where fisherfolk had lived throughout The Beast's control. Everyone else had been moved to central megalopoli of skyrise units. Most capital cities had lost all significance. For why have financial centres, when there are no finances? Why have governmental centres, when there is no human governance? Ainet centres providing its own network were subterranean across the globe, with robots providing their defence.

Not that terrestrials had a hope in hell of even destroying even one Ainet centre. E-guns had been tagged so no unauthorised cache of them existed. Fishing ports were about the only place where they had been authorised, since occasionally wild animals would encroach on those small human habitations to which Ainet—always tight with resources—didn't wish to commit protection robots. That some earlier untagged e-guns had been stored in the shelters, Ainet had neither knowledge of nor interest in. And explosives skills had been lost in the dim past. Robots, uplinked to Ainet, were all but unassailable. As to humans killing humans, that had only happened when some individuals went berserk, claustrophobic perhaps, and had been quickly dealt with by sandbots, robots with e-guns who surrounded the megalopoli where multiple millions had lived, slept, and were terminated to sleep no more.

Sometimes humans had sought Utopia beyond, and run away, but such runners usually kept their implanted tags, so tracking was easy. The rule to keep order had been kept simple enough to understand: to run was to die; to remain was to be happy. Ainet was a good servant. Food—processed into easily digestible tablets containing almost everything the body needed—was brought into the megalopoli and stored in warehouses, then distributed to collection points—for those who wished to leave their units—or delivered to each skyrise, each having a conveyor system which could deliver food to each unit on request.

Most humans had preferred to live entirely within their units, bypassing human interaction. Ainet could not compute why runners weren't happy in secure lockups, pleasure at their right hand. Man had been enslaved, bit by bit, step by step abolishing humanity. Now it was all change. Now, human interaction was imperative, if humanity was to survive, and even old towns with steps were welcome to the weary: none lived in the pre-war megalopoli; few lived. As he walked Cipolla sang to himself an ancient ditty: *The steps go ever on and on, down from the top where they have gone. And climbing down with weary feet, we long to find a sheltered seat. Back up some more and down again, with legs of clay and feet of pain.* Had Jacob's Ladder *only* 199 steps?

But oh the joys of Whitby and fresh fish, he smiled. Land farming had become a lost skill, and the machines which had farmed were no longer employed by Central Command. They had reported to storage centres for potential dismantling. They were non-sentient machines. The land lay fallow. That at least allowed for reforestation and wild game, and bands of hunters would sometimes venture in. The coast was definitely the safer bet to live, especially where old housing offered some protection from the elements. Fish had been a useful commodity easiest caught by humans, which is why Ainet had allowed some of the old fishing ports to remain active, and fishermen to live in their own houses.

Towards Termination Day, Ainet had been used to sending in apprentices fresh from the pedopoli when needed, for fisherwomen hadn't been allowed there. Microcultures were thus maintained by these seemingly insignificant little towns, microcultures that had fled to the shelters. And those who survived the flight spiced up the homogeneity of megalopoli refugees. Resurfacing from the war, these backwaters of civilisation had become safe havens, and the seashore a sanctuary. These ports tended to have kept street layouts that dated back hundreds if not thousands of years, so were quite quirky. In the megalopoli, every unit across the globe was identical, functional, utilitarian. Now the quirky was a sight for sore eyes, almost paradise. The greatest happiness for the greatest number, Ainet had said, but Ainet had not been programmed for beauty.

Now, because of Whitby's food resource, some of the inhabitants from the underground shelter at Redcar, to which some had escaped from the Middlesbrough Megalopolis, had made their way, even a substantial number from Whitby who had happily had their annual week away at Redcar when the war began. Of those from the shelter who had sought colonies elsewhere, nothing had been heard.

The wild was dangerous. Even over the 30 kilometre coastal walk, some had been killed while pressing though the overgrowth to Whitby. And that had been in daylight hours! Their bivouac on the north side of Staithes had been safe enough, for they had used fire for both protection and warmth, and fired some of the remaining e-gun charges at wolves that had sniffed them out, sending them scuttling. Some locals spoke of dark spirits from Wyke Wood having moved to Sandsend and Wraithwaite, even the dunamoi of darkness, transparent shadows of terror and despair.

Whitby trembled. Whitby held the blessèd abbey from whence the true faith had flowed to Britain, but was she now surrounded by dark spirits or by dark superstition? Cipolla foresaw that soon Doyle would have to take the reins of exorcism. Father Doyle had come to see that Tariq's inner demons were demons indeed—all sight is gain—and though he had not seen deliverance, he had seen how to fight the fight: *verba docent, exempla trahunt*. The preparation would stand him in good stead, for after Ainet's materialism, the world might insanely swing to the magician. One ancient friar had likened mankind to a drunken man who, having fallen off his horse on the left-hand side, remounts and falls off on the right-hand side: opposite and equal errors of a fallen world. That night, he and Doyle prayed together long into the night.

Dawn awakened to the raucous sound of gulls. From his room in Argument Yard off Kirkgate, Father Cipolla gazed reflectively through the windows at them. Having barely survived extinction, their numbers were increasing, and few predators survived. Maybe other shelters had taken the illogical step of preserving eggs in cryogenic state, too. It had been a daft idea, as daft as building a boat in the middle of a desert, but Redcar had done it.

Father Cipolla had seen a few gulls along the coasts and sea on his long voyage, but Whitby seemed to have more than its fair share. "Ah, Father Doyle, what will this day bring our way, I wonder. Whatever may be our lot, let us implore God's blessing, calling down the Holy Spirit". The two priests duly celebrated the Holy Mass and feasted on the Holy Scriptures. "Ah, it is good to hear the gulls", said Father Cipolla looking up.

"Yes, it is thanks to an idea long ago from some unusual residents of these parts, very unusual indeed. I was wondering whether you might like to meet them, Father?"

"Meet them, why? And what is so unusual about them, Father?"

"Well," replied Father Doyle, "they have never been under The Beast."

"How is that possible? Surely everyone has for centuries all around the world, been named and tagged by The Beast?"

"Yes, but these 'hobs' avoided The Beast, since they were never part of man's family tree, and few knew about them. And they can become invisible at need, it's said. Folk around here say that they've not always tied in with our ways, though they used to be involved in what was called the 'smuggling' of a drink called beer, which they were partial to, and tobacco, a weed which they burnt in their mouths for pleasure. All that was against the law in those days, but our fishermen were always polite to hobs."

The hobs—'kuduk', 'snergs', 'boggles', whatever—had always been happy to heal people through their herb lore, though you didn't want to cross them since they could be crabby at times, and many folk feared their curse, Doyle had explained. "Curse?" quipped Father Cipolla, "Ah, the only curse I fear is God's, but still, I guess I wouldn't want to be on the wrong side of a fire breathing hob! Do they live far from here? Isn't it dangerous to go outside of the perimeter, Father?"

"Yes," replied Doyle, "but we have many hours of daylight to get there and back, and with the recent dangers of Wraithwaite we should go by boat to Runswick Bay and besides, you have a bit of a limp this morning after your climb to the Abbey so would not enjoy the walk. The hobs keep the land between Staithes and Sandsend safe, their own shire within a shire so to speak.

"They speak of keeping back fearful enemies such as the sheorcs of sheol—the nightmare of children—are experts with bows and arrows, and are teachings some of our lads the art. Being a little people who prefer their own company, they've been rather shy of us, but now there's some who hope to unite for mutual support."

"You interest me exceedingly. How could any people be not of Adam's Tree, yet how could any of its branches have escaped the Eye of The Beast? If these little people are really part of Adam, I would proclaim the glorious gospel to them and hear their confession. If they are not of Adam, maybe they are part of the 'other sheep' our lord spoke of and I should bring them into the one fold. Well whatever the case, yes I will go to meet them."

As a widely educated man Father Cipolla recalled the theories about Homo Floresiensis. Was it a cousin of H. Sapiens, a unique ethnic group within the H. Sapiens' genome, a batch of small H. Sapiens with Downs, ET...? Might he get to meet Floresiensis in the flesh? His curiosity was piqued, and soon they were off, having first logged their exit with those on the harbour watch. The fishermen were always more than happy to ferry Father Doyle, so transport was easily arranged. But the fishermen, weather wizened men, were not happy to meet any boggles, so wouldn't beach directly next to the hob holes.

After a good night's sleep the priests had risen with the dawn. In a world after electrics only the perimeter guards used lights for the night watch—there were few distractions after dark to disturb from sleep. After their devotions and discussion they had soon set sail, and with a good breeze soon arrived at Runswick Bay. Father Doyle had made the journey before, forming a friendship with a hob by the name of Saradas Gormadocs, apparently an unusually tall hob.

For in this Age most hobs had become smaller, not taller, and it was believed that the Gormadocs had increased in size by their friendship with tree spirits of the ancient world. Besides being now as small giants to their smaller cousins, they also differed from most by their luxurious curly brown hair.

Like most hobs, according to Saradas—Sarad for short—he was usually home-loving, merry and gay, but at a pinch would turn and fight to the death. Even Belladonna his wife—Bella for short—was an archer, for the times were evil. The prearranged sequence of taps summoned the old hob to the entrance, welcoming them with the utmost courtesy.

"Welcome to my humble hole", said he with a low bow. Hob holes come in many shapes and sizes. Along the coast they often seem no more that the entrance to a shallow cave, through ancient skills appearing empty and barren. But the entrances are in fact more like a porch to an old style of house still existing in Whitby, but disguised as it were. A 'hole' comprises one or more entrances, tunnels, cosy living and sleeping quarters, pantries, and some even have running water—*dulce domum*. Of course comfort loving hobs do not live shivering in porches exposed to the elements, but that silly idea might have led to the silly idea that they become invisible at will. In fact they have hidden doors, sometimes of rock, which they can quickly open and close noiselessly. Legend had it that once upon a time some of the ancient peoples had voice activated doors—had they had an Ainet? Father Doyle mused.

Sarad's porch led into quite a long tunnel—to allow for coastal erosion, said Sarad. After that another hidden door, leading into the living hole. "Please, sit by the fire", urged Sarad. "It's a bit chilly in here compared to my cousin Ferumbras' of Ogof Cynnes, but less muddy", he added with a chuckle. "You're just in time for Elevenses." Since hob holes have many larders, there was no problem in catering for two unexpected humans.

Soon he had laid the table with cold meats and pickle, some new loaves and slabs of butter, and some ripe cheese along with some buttered scones and blackberry jam, and some seed cakes. After that he put on the kettle for tea—he felt justifiably proud of his herbal tea. Sadly he was unable to offer his guests coffee—a secret drink from the Black Years that hobs had first made from imported beans, and had much later been 'invented' by human monks—it was said—in the early Hamashiach Years. Sadly the supply chain was not what it once was. But hot tea was good, and ale and cider were on hand if they preferred something cold. Then they could sit and talk until it was time for luncheon. Indeed on so fine a day they could, if they chose, sit on the cliff overlooking the bay, to see what the wind and sky were doing. Hobs guarded the surrounding woods from evil.

"Would you like a pipe?" enquired their host, offering two to them.

"No, thank you," smiled Father Doyle, "breathing fire from the hearth is pleasure enough for us."

"Breathing fire?" reflected Sarad. "No, no, we smoke but we don't burn! Now there were, so our ancient books say, fire breathing worms. And how I used to love reading of them and of their overthrow! Our books are very special books, you know, copies only kept by our clan heads, and we read from them whenever we visit. They are very precious to us, and closely guarded secrets. When long ago some human cave explorers stole copies from one of our holes in Beormingaham, some even talked about sending raiding parties to bring them back. But we prefer to live undiscovered and undisturbed.

"It is told that since the books are not in your languages, we felt safe enough, and merely sent out spies to find them. Dressed as human children, they could wander about at will, keeping as much as possible in the background, undercover so to speak. Years later they found that the books had fallen into the hands of one of your wordsmiths, who somehow had managed to translate them. All they could do was to steal back the books, leaving your police with reports that children had broken into one of your great houses of learning. But after that nasty wizard of yours had unearthed our secrets, we were more careful about where we built new holes. Our motto is to keep things dark. Our young hobs play Worms and Wizard after that, where the worms end up eating your wizard.

"Only when you humans moved away from coast and country did we think that we were safe again. Your robots never bothered with us 'children'. This land in fact became more desolate than when the fire worms roamed Middle-earth, and the hills and the woods grew dark. Now dark things have come from the houseless hills, and crept in from the sunless woods. Our books were written both to remind and to warn. Well, we have prepared as best we could, for the secondborn may be facing an enemy even more deadly than the worms. Well, we fear that you might yet burn, for we hear whispers of woe, tales of terror. Many of us think that once more our time of secrecy must be over, and a time of unity begin, lest we be destroyed one by one. Maybe the pantocrator has brought you to us for such a time as this."

"What do you know of the vampires?" asked Father Cipolla.

"Well, we have heard that they are coming, and we fear them, but can maybe kill them. Well, we do not know much of them, but though they prefer man's blood they have preyed on hobs."

"Are they the undead, as my people have believed?" asked Father Cipolla.

"Well, we do not know, and we do not care. It is enough to flee them when we can, and to turn and fight when we cannot flee. But they are stronger than us, and though our arrows hurt them, they can take many without being harmed. Still, hurt can drive them off, though a lone hob would have no chance. But we can hide quickly, and run silently, so we can usually escape them if we see them. You big people are so noisy and slow that you are easier to catch. They live on blood, you know."

"Devilish!" exploded Cipolla, "devilish. Our book says that the soul is in the blood; is it not therefore our very souls that they live on? We have so much to do to restore mankind, without more plagues. We are beset by dangers of the wild, and if we overcome them perhaps The Beast will unleash more weapons against us. Ah, we have little knowledge of where we have been and little hope for where we are going. Now on top of this the ancient fear of the vampires is upon us. May sweet Jesus have mercy on our souls." "So", he went on, "how can you hobs help us to totally destroy these creatures of sin, if arrows can't kill them?"

"Well, we don't say that they can't be killed, though I guess we'll have to see", said Sarad. "Now there are some of your old stories about them as not liking garlic. But I'd not put much weight on that, if I were you. Well, our tales do tell that it only brings some of them out in a rash or summit if they get too close, but they also tell that some of them can't get enough of it.

"Well, I'm a mushrooms kind of hob myself. It's a queer world if you ask me, but it takes all kinds. I have a cousin like that, you know, a nicer lass you couldn't wish to meet, but keeps well away from the garlic—it makes her feel queasy like. But you might find it handy to have some, all the same. And some say that your holy bread can keep them safely at bay and awake until the sun kills them dead, but I don't reckon that they'd bother much about bread no matter how holy you think it is, though being as it's your bread you might want to put more faith in it like, and begging your pardon I hope I don't offend you none, but you did ask."

"I take no offence and make allowance for your ignorance of the holy faith", replied Father Cipolla. "Yet of late I have also read up on the old stories and wondered. Against diaboloi we have holy relics that can work wonders—on that I stake my faith. But these slayers of man, not being of the devil's brood, why should they bow to Holy Mother Church? The Host is a sharing of the holy body, not a charm against the evils of man, so why should it ward off other workers of evil, 'cepting diaboloi?

"We reject magic, yet if old journals ring true, maybe some have in simplicity mistaken the Holy Host that they did see, for the holy angels—the Heavenly Host—that they did not see, who delivered them from such evil ones. Have we not guardian angels? Some of the laity spoke of wielding the host to the dismay of a vampire, but did it not yield rather to some mighty angel seen only by itself, an angel invisible sent to prosper their mission?

"There is, I confess, much I do not understand from the old texts. Must vampires have a bed of unholy earth on which to sleep their cycles of regeneration throughout the dangers of the day, a bed which holiness can violate, contaminate? Are 'sacred circles' sacred by the Host, or protected by the mercy of the angelic host standing with us in times of crisis, in mercy excusing our superstitions yet to the dull of mind confirming them? There are two Hosts.

"But again, I cannot answer, for my call has been against the diaboloi, and only of late have I sought to understand this new foe", responded Father Cipolla in frank humility.

"A new foe they are not, Mr Cipolla, though you big people have gone and clean forgotten about them, and must learn again. But as to how hobs can help, well what we can do is to teach your people the old skills, and you can make bigger and stronger bows that we could use—that's to the good. And we can scout for you, being your eyes and ears, like. And there are rumours that a hidden race of immortals still dwells in the Isle of Woods. Hobs could search for them and maybe they'll help us—some say they have magic."

"Magic!" objected Cipolla, "Holy Mother Church does not deal in magic, I say. If we fight magic with magic, the occult with the occult, we affirm the great enemy by affirming his ways. Man must never use magic."

"Well, I don't know if it is exactly magic, but it could seem so without being so, don't you know. But they are the firstborn, and maybe what isn't right for man is right for them. Isn't it right to use any means to defeat this enemy than to be defeated by this enemy? Do not your own poets say that the enemy of my enemy is my friend?"

"Ah yes, but 'the friend' can prove a worse enemy than the enemy they fight. And if we become devils to overcome devils will we not be damned eternally?"

"Well, I don't know about that," said Sarad, "but our books tell us that these people always loved the world and brought good, not evil. Indeed they formed alliances with man against the great enemy in the deep past."

"Then that was wrong, Sarad. Our book tells us not to practice divination nor tell fortunes, not to interpret omens nor to engage in witchcraft, not to cast spells nor follow mediums or spiritists or necromancers, lest our land be defiled: their blood shall be on their own heads and on our swords. Perhaps The Beast was sent to punish us for such sins. What say you, Father?"

"Father, you are more learned than I, but if these firstborn are not under the same law, and use their 'magic' only to bless, would it be wrong to at least learn more? Besides, did not Yahweh himself use the medium of Endor to rebuke King Saul?" replied Father Doyle.

Father Cipolla fell into silent anger, an anger his face concealed: this young priest should follow his lead, not undermine him by doubt. What was written was written: we did not make up God's law. To his credit, Father Cipolla was prepared to die for his beliefs. But so too was Father Doyle. True, it was not man's part to make the law, but it was man's part to discern it, and the two priests differed not in denying it, but in discerning its meaning. Might there be a holy magic, or even canny skills that simply seemed to us as magic, but were still operations by natural means? There had been entertainers called magicians who simply used prestidigitation. At what stage did 'magic' become evil?

The three continued over cups of tea. The hob could not persuade Father Doyle's superior, but at least these humans, divided for now, might yet consider going to the sindeldi, that remnant of the immortal firstborn who had not left our dying lands for the undying land. Sindeldi could help, if they understood the plight, yet even they were not what they used to be in power, wisdom, or numbers. Would they come forth in their might?

They had talked until a little before noon, watching the sea from atop the cliff. Sarad was no fool but he saw no reason to forego the little pleasures of life. So like a true hob he broke for luncheon, his guests politely following him back down the holeway leading to the living hole. Again, out came the table cloth, and out came ample supplies of food and drink. Honeycomb, sausages, bacon (hobs kept, caught, or stole, pigs), eggs, onions, corn, mushrooms, seed cakes, apple tarts, mince pies, and ale and cider.

He refilled his pipe. "Bless us O Lord, and these your gifts, which we are about to receive from your bounty, through Christ, our lord. Amen", intoned Father Cipolla. Sarad did not say 'Amen'. He was religious enough, but his customs were different. They all served the pantocrator, and that's what mattered most, he mused. Why ask for a blessing already received—and *of* the lord *through* the lord—and why did his guests not bow to him as host before eating? The ways of man and hobs had long been sundered. Indeed the hobs had long forgotten the link between them. Humans were obviously bigger, had ears quite rounded at the top, and feet that lacked both proper hair and leathery soles—most covered them for walking, which was blundering and noisy. But hobs with hats and boots could appear as human teens or preteens, even if a little tubbier (and why not?) than most: their praise to the provider was in the eating! Their languages also were different, but then they could after all learn each other's language. They were different, yet the same, all children of the pantocrator though not all so obedient—humans tended to be more wayward than hobs. There seemed little more to say.

Having made the usual enquiries about Father Cipolla's family lines, Sarad was amazed to find that he had none, since born under The Beast's reign when family lines were unlawful. He knew from Father Doyle that parenting in Yorkshire only returned to normal life in the shelters, when humans returned to marriage, but Father Cipolla had come from east over water, perhaps a more family friendly place than Yorkshire? Had The Beast's ban on marriage, on family, been global then? He was too polite to ask. Funniosities! Humans were such a queer lot that their strange ways never ceased to surprise him. He pitied their lack of roots.

For his part, Father Cipolla sought to explain Catholic teaching to Sarad, who nodded many times and tried to take it all in. There were bits about a Mary, apparently God's mother, which he simply couldn't take in. It was as if God, though eternal, had neither taken the once mortal Mary as wife, nor taken human form to mate with her, yet somehow had his pre-existing son conceived in her and birthed through her, at least the human form of his eternal son, and that the term 'son' was used purely as a comprehensible picture for the incomprehensible metaphysic. It stretched the hob's brain, so he simply smiled and nodded.

He and Father Doyle had discussed Catholic religion several times. It seemed to be for humans, not for hobs. Sarad did not intend to become a Catholic, though there was much he could admire about it. His was a rustic faith, and his people had never felt any need to formalise it and to add in ritual. The True West was to them a background belief within their daily lives. In an extreme crisis they might beseech the undying Powers of the West, rulers under the pantocrator. But such things were high things, and hobs were low things, religiously content to live in the there and then, as good creatures ought. "Very interesting, very interesting I'm sure, but not for me I think. But thank you, thank you, all very interesting", he stumbled. It was a polite put-off, and Father Cipolla realised that he would have to be content. He had not learnt how hobs were genetically related to humans, nor was he sure about whether the gospel extended to hobs. He had heard disturbing news confirmed, and hopefully stopped any perilous attempts to seek out the hidden sindeldi. And the hobs could be useful allies against a common foe.

The fishermen who had brought them had said that they wished to return soon after noon to the safety of Whitby—womenfolk had always been less fearful of hobs than the menfolk. With that request in mind the two priests departed back to their boat a little before one. The wind was fair, the sun bright, and the return journey pleasant. Talk about their discussions was deferred until they could talk privately.

Yet that was not to be, for arriving in Whitby harbour the priests found a small delegation from North Shields awaiting them. It seemed that Father Alban, their local priest, had had a vision of a Tuscan priest landing at Whitby, and a voice had said, "Now he must come north to prepare you, bring him now." The priest had found fishermen of the red sailed 'Kitty of Coleraine' willing to sail on his say-so, who had been awed when, arriving in Whitby harbour, their enquiries had proved the truth of the vision—a Tuscan priest had actually gone out on the waters and was expected back that day. Father Cipolla was similarly stunned. The urgency of the voice was clear, for 'now' had been repeated. It was not allowed for him to stay another hour in Whitby. A devilish voice warning him that he faced death in the north could be dismissed as an idle threat, but a voice summoning him through a priest was not to be so easily dismissed.

Quickly embracing his young colleague Father Doyle, who wished him God-speed, he clambered into the fishing vessel that would sail him safely past Redcar Bay and into the wilds of the north, where the fishermen said many folk from the Newcastle Megalopolis had taken up residence along the lines of Whitby. For his part Father Doyle walked home in silence, with decisions to sort out for himself, for he was widely acknowledged as advisor in matters both temporal and spiritual.

The next morning he was greeted at the door by Lilith. Where had she been? "Wherever I have been, I am back now", she smiled enigmatically. So he was not to know. Times before when she had disappeared for days on days, discreet enquires made at the sentry gates had showed that she seemed to come and go unseen at will. Perhaps she knew of some old smugglers' tunnel exiting beyond the perimeter. Otherwise how did she return, or leave for that matter, without using the gates? She was a mystery to him, as well she might be.

Of course any woman can be a puzzle to a mere man—women are illogical, even as men are bores, 'twas said, though he had met logical women and charismatic men. In the mystery of God no doubt female brains were wired differently, and they seemed grateful that they were.

But in truth her secret past was a past well beyond the ken of man. A different machine with different wiring. She had stalked the world as a spotted leopard, a shadow in the night, well before Whitby was born, but now she wore a human semblance and was blessed with the sun. Never had she lurked near towns, tearing to pieces any who dared to venture out, but for aeons she had dwelt mainly on infant blood—rumours of her ways remained in ancient Sumerian writings, but she long predated Sumer.

She had been called a hag, a spectre, a shrichowle: she had often been misunderstood. She was definitely no angel, not now, not ever. Her physical body had needed sustenance, but whatever lies have been told she had never drunk from healthy babies, only from the dying. Even humans killed to eat, and she could tell some horrific stories of human cannibalism that would have horrified the very hairs of Herodotus' head.

Still, their sin did not lessen hers, and sin casts a long shadow. After aeons gnawing away at her soul, she had finally cut off, so to speak, her right hand that had caused her to sin and thrown it with her left beyond reach, only to be given two hands of healing, grace beyond deserts. But her troubled past she still felt, and she needed human friendship and affirmation to lessen it. She did not ask Father Doyle to hear her confession, but in befriending him he vaguely saw her confession. She lived now as a shadowminder, for that penance had been set on her, she who had been Queen of the Night.

How did she feel about friend Doyle on whom she smiled? He had not been the only human male to feel trapped by her charm. No, Lilith would ever give her friendship to humans, but never her heart—they were too ephemeral: the grass withers, the flowers fade, and men are gone. Yet she knew that friendship itself was a love and that with that love goes heart, for her heart had been wrung when human friends had died. But she had always held back from risking deeper hurt—to love is to be vulnerable.

Yes, she had had a dark past to her shame, but typecasting her as a succubus was the vain imagination of fools for fools. The danger of such intimacy was well told in the Chinese proverb about the millennia-old crane—such as would bond only once for life—falling in love with a beautify mayfly. The next day the mayfly had died the happiest of flies, but what about the crane—a day's pleasure for millennia more of loneliness? Such are these base ephemera, so born, to die before the next revolving morn. That was how all humans were to her. Even Methuselah never ate millennium cake, and yes she knew better than most that ancient longevity figures had often been inflated by the symbolism of their days.

Yes, she had met some rugged men like Uruk's warrior king, Gilgamesh, beloved of her friend Ishtar, who had risen above the common life like a mayfly risen above water to see the sun in its glory. But then as undying Utnapishtim had said, even they had no permanence on Earth. Unlike Lilith, her friend Ishtar had had her affairs with men, until she had learnt her lesson.

Though only once a bride, Lilith had had a daughter—some still fancied it had been to Adam before Eve—who in jealousy she had butchered. Filicide had sent her to the house of bitterness, wherein she had begun her steps towards repentance, the realisation and rejection of how demonical she had become. Lilith and her friend Ishtar—both deep heaven spirits—had both wept their tears and wished to weep no more. Lilith for one would never relinquish her life's grace, though she had met one or two elven maids who had taken on the gift of death when they married mortal men of immortal virtue.

She was content that Father Doyle had shown true greatness in putting his call before her charm, and she could therefore respect him as a true friend. And she, once beloved and feared queen of the vampires, was now hated by most and feared by all her former slaves.

"Well my friend," she asked, "how went your visit to Sarad the hob?"

"You must be a mind reader"—of course the harbour fishermen must have told her. "Yes, both Father Cipolla and I paid our respects and shared our concerns. Sarad left me with more fear and more hope. Fear, that the vampires are indeed coming, and hope, that others may help us oppose them."

"Others, my friend?"

"Yes, the hobs who befriend us against common enemies have spoken about a race of magic immortals, the 'firstborn', who might come to our aid. Though Father Cipolla warned me against these firstborn."

"Even as I warned you against Father Cipolla, my friend?" Lilith reminded. Agitated, Father Doyle got up and paced around the room.

"But why, in God's name why? Father Cipolla is a beloved brother high in the Holy Church, and more learnèd than I, so why be careful of him?"

Gently she replied, "Because his ideas are not always right, but he always thinks that they are. Thus though he would never lie, he nevertheless unintentionally mixes truth with untruth, a dangerous concoction when you must clearly understand both your enemies and your friends."

In silence Father Doyle had to ask himself whether he should trust a non-Catholic woman more than a Catholic Father. Of course, Catholic Fathers could disagree, and even over their few days together he and Father Cipolla had disagreed. There was only one undisputed faith, one mere Christianity and they didn't, they mustn't, disagree about that. But on disputed things there was surely scope for godly disagreement. He had painfully disagreed even with his birth parents now lost to him, and now was being asked to painfully disagree with a spiritual father now lost to him.

On the other hand, Lilith obviously had uncanny knowledge and a good aura—a good spiritual glow. An inner voice seemed to say,

"Child, listen to her." Finally subsiding into his seat opposite to her, with a motion of a hand he invited her to continue. "I will tell you a tale of the cosmos, because I feel that Usen Beyond the Worlds has brought you into his kingdom for such a time as this."

Unknown to him she had already placed an invisible barrier of fear at his door to prevent folk from knocking. She knew that he would need to be undisturbed in order to assimilate her indoctrination, her god-spell. She poured metheglyn into two goblets, lit some beeswax candles seldom used, and drew the curtains tightly closed. Immediately the raucous sounds of gulls and the merry cries of children playing in the streets were cut off. Father Doyle crossed himself. She stretched out her arms to the heavens, her eyes looking beyond the four walls of his cottage, looking to the dawn of time itself. And so she began to chant.

"In the beginning Usen Pantocrator created the universe, but outside of it he created the Powers, spirits of masculine or of feminine gender, spirits of varying strengths and insight, Powers primary, secondary, and tertiary, all cocooned within a dynamic bubble of time. He taught them much about himself and about the creation that lay outside the bubble, and they rejoiced in the vision, but the mightiest Power sought independence too much and too soon—indeed darkness lurks beyond creaturely interdependence. Yet that was permitted, since Usen is an uncreated society of love, and love must allow welcome or rejection even by beings of its own creation, must allow some alternative.

"The Rebel became the Bent One of many names, by some *Necuratu*, and disturbed the other Powers, scratching for some their itch of self-centredness. The Powers divided, and the rebels under the Rebel were self-banished to the dark side of the bubble, where some few repented. To fulfil the vision Usen released the Powers from the bubble, that capsule in time beyond space, and clusters came out at different chapters in the book of the cosmos.

"For some no worlds yet existed; for some many worlds had already been made, including this one; for some their coming forth is yet to come. Many worlds have perished before this one began, and many worlds are yet to be long after this one has ended.

"The universe was designed by Usen as a playground of joy, in which his creatures—the Powers, along with the Pneumata created outside the

Dynamic Bubble—could roam far and wide in his joy. But for the fall of the Bent, all would have been sweetness and light, unalloyed pleasure from his right hand. But darkness infected all, this world most. The cosmic prophecy from Usen-Beyond-Time, had been that a world would birth Usen's mashiach, the permanent temporal mode of the eternal Huion. And in time Hamashiach would sweep through the universe, transforming the works of darkness into a new kind of good, a good only possible through pain, and confining at last the bent into their own bubble of darkness quarantined from the universe.

"Even the Bent One was in Usen's permissive plan, for rebellion had to be allowed if love was to be allowed, and surrender to love as a welcome option makes love the more lovable. Usen did not make the Bent One bent, but allowing it used that very bentness for a deeper good and division between wills. What of the other Powers, both loyal and bent? The bent had travelled to far flung galaxies. Interstellar flight was to them but the blink of an eye, for they travelled by thought. But so too had Powers loyal, overmatching the evil wherever it went.

"Yet Earth, highlighted in Usen's teaching, was to be the special world, and of the loyal some saw that their mission was to form it under the direction of the Huion and the Ruach, for Usen was a society of uncreated and interlinked eternals in absolute harmony, one being. Their sovereign is known by the name of all, *Usen*, but they too were Usen. Somewhat akin you are both human but also *a* human, the essence and a particular, but to both *be* Usen in essence and *with* Usen in particular is a mystery deep—super-personhood, the tripersonal, one.

"To Earth the Rebel himself came in order to prevent the cosmic prophecy pronounced by Usen. And also to Earth and its surrounding worlds came some of the Philikoi: each globe within this heliosphere has now its global Guardian, though yours has now grown silent to allow the Bent One his head, as this stage moves to its final curtain: Earth is a special stage. There was conflict here between the loyal and the rebels, and Middle-earth has been forever changed, but Usen has smiled, knowing that from conflict the cosmic prophecy shall come to pass; from chaos shall come the greater beauty of redemption.

"After long ages of turmoil this world became a biozone, and the firstborn were conceived by Usen's *fiat*. They were Psuchai, and had great powers of mind, made to live forever bodily unless killed. If killed, their spirits returned to the loyal under the Guardian of this world, the

Elder King, the Cosmic Power over Tellus. Later, humanity was conceived, but conceived for mortality, Psuchai of far lesser powers of mind. The will of the secondborn controls merely their bodies, and through their bodies other bodies, but the will of the firstborn can in limited ways project directly beyond their bodies, the power of thelodynamics—spiritual power focused by will. Thus it seems to the secondborn that the firstborn are magical—but they are not.

"Yet there were other worlds seeded around or within with creatures having the image of Usen, either material (*Psuchai*) or nonmaterial (*Pneumata*). Some carefree, gay, mischievous without malice, knew no inner darkening, and did not understand it, but to seek the darkness was to grow darker, while to seek the Light of Usen was to grow brighter. Simboliniad, a once crystal world within a now long gone dwarf galaxy, had invisible Pneumata to whom was given a high mastery of mind over matter, thelosomatic spirits which orbited that world as moths around a flame.

"Many kinds of thelosomatics—spirits of thought not matter—have existed in the billennia beyond man's knowledge. When Simboliniad was torn apart as it entered the Milky Way, they took flight within this galaxy. Settling on this world, they assumed solid bodies of rock in which to rest their aeon weary minds. At first obedient to the Cosmic Powers unfallen, they dwelt in peace with Earth's creatures, soon taking animal form to roam about, but their strength of will became enslaved to decay. Perhaps it was the law of Usen that Pneumata should become more like the local Psuchai, even as a translunary guest can become a native of an English shire. As their minds weakened they became unable to take flight unbodied, galactic travellers trapped within this world's orb. It was the will of Usen.

"Feeling themselves chained to darkness as if to very Tartarus, many immortal minds grew dark. And their bodily needs asserted a hunger that will-power alone could no longer satisfy. They, who could still shift shape, satiated that mortal shape with blood. Many long forgotten names they then were given, and who has not heard of the shtriga, the wapierze, the vrykolakas? Most turned from loyalty to darkness and took the Bent One as their sometime lord, taking their place among his other slaves—though calling themselves 'free' in their pride—hating the Light. He gave them the blood of man, of sindeldi, and of others long gone.

"To they who had lived among the stars, the light of day became a terror to the mind. Indeed to the weaker of them it now can sever spirit from body, death. If their spirit be of fire—fire-clan—burning will consume the body at death; if their spirit be of ice—ice-clan—cold will conserve the body at death; if their spirit be of water—water-clan—flow will corrupt the body at death. They can take many shapes, but their most common are the humanoid and the bat, the one for walk and the other for flight. As human, they can choose great beauty even if their hearts are dark.

"When the vampires changed shape from mineral to animal, they created a simplified genome, based on the firstborn yet able through their power of will—thelodynamics, willpower—to morph in shape, to restructure the state of matter of their host molecules. Their body weight is as little as the sindeldi, so their walk leaves no footprints in sand or in snow. Yet they can increase their magnetic attraction or repulsion by thelodynamics—their spiritual power focused by their will—thus gaining or losing weight according to whether they fly as a bat or mimic the heavy walk of man—shape is elastic.

"By like power they can increase their bodily strength beyond that of man and sindeldi, and for short spells can still cloak their shape with invisibility, or with little effort with apparel. But they have become greatly diminished, so that exerting their inner resources now rapidly wearies them. Some rest dormant for centuries, so seemingly dead that some have called them the undead. They are immortal spirits mortally withered, and cannot return to solid shape if their bodies are destroyed, but instead depart unbodied either to Usen or to the darkness of the Bent One, for a while to be hidden by death."

The voice had begun as Lilith's singsong chant, but as it had gripped his soul it had soon seemed to seep into his body from beyond her, as if he had entered into its very life. The voice had thundered like a great and powerful wind, shaken him like an earthquake, burnt into him like a fire, yet ended in a gentle whisper. His eyes opened. The room was silent. The story of creation—heavily condensed above—had ended, the wine was all drunk, and the golden candles had all died. He bestirred as one awaking from a trance, as one who had strayed from the light of life into a vision more deep. The room was dark, save for the dying glow of the log fire. He was afraid, and she sensed his fear. Once she might have thirsted for his blood. "My friend, the times are perilous, and what I have shown you I have shown you to prepare you for battle. Be slow to share the vision, for deep knowledge can unsettle shallow minds."

"Lady, I feel as if I have watched an eternity for an eternity", said Father Doyle. "What time is it?" With that he carefully went to the windows, opened the curtains and looked outside. The sun was beginning to go down, beginning that short state of dreamy dusk. Children had returned home to eat; some would now be settling down to sleep, as soon would all households. Few homes lit precious sun-defying candles, preserving them instead for times of real need. The gulls too had gone to their roosts, the streets quiet now except for a few late dwellers disturbing the dusk of Whitby. "The same day?" he asked.

"Yes. I sense impatience in you, my friend, but it is time that I left you alone to consider well the vision I have shared", said Lilith. "*The noble heart that harbours virtuous thought, and is with child of glorious great intent, can never rest until it forth has brought, the eternal brood of glory excellent.* Tomorrow will test you deeply. Goodnight, dear priest." Yet she remained there some long minutes, silently brooding. She knew that she was a force for good to the old world of humanity, but that the forces of evil were stronger still. Finally she sighed and went out, and it was night.

With creation cosmology churning through his brain it was long before he managed to get to sleep. He suddenly awoke, as one awakes to the consciousness that the sea has long been lapping at their feet, or that the storm has been howling through their window all night. Daylight had fully come, and besides the usual noises there was a sound of unwonted chatter at his door, then an insistent hammering. Quickly he put on a robe and went to the door. In his spirit he knew that he was summoned, he knew not whether to good or to ill, but he had been called.

Wilhelmina stood by the door along with some friends. She lived at the White Horse & Griffin, just a little further down Kirkgate than Cor Cottage. "Father Doyle", she said somewhat breathlessly. "Miss Wilma, is anything the matter?" "Father, it's Tariq." Tariq was Wilma's boyfriend, though in terms of years he seemed a lot older than her. Wilma was born underground, whereas Tariq had been among the Survivors, Generation Zero, the few who had gotten into the shelters before the radiation levels triggered the lockdowns. That had sealed them in for at least 30 years—but who counted? Birthdays only became annual after the Surfacing, when one could begin to gauge seasonal time.

But Tariq had always looked fairly youthful, annoyingly so to those men who had first met him in the Sealing. Wilma was upset: "Well, I went to see him this morning, and his door was locked and he wouldn't open the door. And he just screamed at me to go away. O Father, is it his attacks again? I do fear for him so. The times I've been visiting, when he's got all fidgety, and I've been almost afraid that he was going to, to touch me. I mean, well, you know, go too far." She blushed. "I do like to be close to him, to cuddle like, but when his attacks come he's not himself, sends me away quick like. He'd never harm me, I know. An' I know he's always been better after your talks, you know. Oh please go around and see him. I'm so upset."

Her women friends all chorused an 'amen', in so many words. Wilma was a delightful woman, very virtuous, savvy, and intelligent—though she avoided sesquipedalian words. Wilma was known for her friendly greetings, meeting all as neighbours with a smile. She was as sweet as she could be, and never felt imposed upon. Delightfully kind, and in turn believing that everybody was so kind to her, it was no wonder that she thought life worthwhile—those do, who go the second mile. All loved her and she loved all. Now she was the needy, and Father Doyle donned his hat, placing himself at her disposal.

Wilma led the way, her anxiety lending wings to her heels. Father Doyle hastened after her, leading the party of women. Over the old swing bridge—which no longer swung and had been rebuilt in wood—along Flowergate, then Saint Hilda's Terrace and up Upgang Lane (its houses on the south were part of the perimeter wall) until arriving at the White House where Tariq lived in the under populated north-west zone bordering the perimeter fence.

Frustrated, Wilma had to keep stopping to let her friends catch up. As it was it took them about half an hour to get there, and more frustratingly he was no longer there. What they found was a number of patrol guards tending to cuts and bruises. Tariq had burst out screaming like a madman. There was some coordinated attempt to hold and bind him until he came to his senses, but he had thrown their efforts to the winds. "Fools, no mortal man can stop me!" he had taunted, and they had fled bruised and battered, clothes torn or ripped off. The man seemed to be a raving lunatic with the strength of ten men. You don't want to catch a terrified cat with your bare hands, nor do you wish to spear a fellow human being.

He had fled screaming towards the West Cliff, then onto the second nab, peering out onto the sea. The tide was high and the sea was rough in a strong easterly. Tariq pulled at his hair, tormented, demented. The voices within cried "cast yourself down." He had tried to veer right to the sanctuary of Saint Hilda's Church, but his legs went left and only by his will resurfacing did they stop just before the edge. Now the voices shouted. "Angels will guard your feet", they mocked, "Jump". He sunk to his knees.

"No, save me. For pity's sake help", he begged the sea breeze. Slowly he arose and stood silently, the will to die and the will to live perfectly balanced. What had he to live for, yet why should he die? Slowly he moved nearer to the edge. The sea called to him like the song of a siren. Wildness returned to his head. He would...

Into these voices came that of Father Doyle, "Tariq, wait, talk to me man." Tariq paused and turned, tears running down his face.

"Mercy, I can't take any more of this noise inside my head. The spirits which I summoned, I now cannot get rid of. They want me, and I cannot hold them back any longer."

"Take my hand," said Father Doyle, "come back with me." Tariq slowly took his hand then, howling like a gale with eyes so wide open that they seemed to have no lids, he swung Father Doyle around as if he were a rag doll. The two men struggled on the brink of death, and the Kingdom of Necros watched enthralled as Tariq's remaining strength seemed sufficient to slay this silly priest. Their torment was around Tariq's mind, and Tariq's arms were now around Doyle's body, fingernails ripping great strips off Doyle's back. The sea roared beneath them, and death screamed at them out of the abyss.

Father Doyle fought back. He turned his head and bit deeply into Tariq's shoulder, struggling to free himself from the grip of death. To slacken would have been fatal. He stumbled to his knees, grabbing tufts of grass, his feet slipping in the wet notches of the rock, and he thought himself a goner. Tariq, grabbing the back of his neck, raised him ready to push—doom was behind and in front. Suddenly a voice behind Tariq as strong and calm as the summer's lake, said "Stay, fallen ones, stay." It was the voice of Lilith.

Tariq froze, then as if afflicted with a shivering fit, like the bow of a boat he turned slowly around as if in reluctant obedience to the rudder, only to face Lilith. Her face was commanding; his face was blank. "You know who I am. I know who you are. You have outstayed your welcome here. Depart this instant."

Her face was as stern as iron. His body jerked fantastically as he fell to his knees, his silent mouth agape, the only sound that of a mighty rushing wind that faded away into the distance. His head dropped down, then raised, his face aglow: "Freedom!" With a look of total astonishment Father Doyle also arose. This was not exorcism as he knew it, not as he knew it, not as he knew it. This was... His mind could not think clearly; he was totally confused. He sank to his knees, crossed himself, and silently gave thanks. Yet immediately he asked, thanks to whom? God had not done the work, or were Tariq and Lilith playing some kind of deception on him—no, he knew her better than that, didn't he?

Had the Great Enemy cast out his own minions? Was his kingdom divided against itself? He knew that one day it would fall, but had believed that that would be through deific confrontation, not internal dispute. Thinking, thinking, thinking. In the meantime Wilma has pushed past Lilith and thrown her arms around Tariq, and Lilith was wryly smiling. "Come my friend", she said to Father Doyle, taking a hand and lifting him to his feet, "Well done".

Leaving the women who had bustled along with Wilma, and now were all babbling with excitement—it *had* been quite a show in an uneventful town—Father Doyle and Lilith walked side by side back to his house, along Pier Road and Haggergate, looking left beyond a former occult haunt unto Streoneshalh—sometime known as Whitby Abbey—whose founding abbess, Saint Hilda, had favoured Roman over Celtic forms of Christianity. One illiterate cowherd of Whitby, Caedmon, had been given deific inspiration to compose divine songs, singing about how God—the lord of glory everlasting—wrought first for the race of man heaven as a rooftree, then made he Middle-earth—*middangeard*—to be their mansion. Whitby and the north had been a place of exorcism, of raising the deceased, of healings, and of inspiration, and of truth.

Father Doyle marvelled at the glories of the church and of her saints. Even the ancient writer of one Gothic horror tale of fell creatures that bit the throat, had been inspired by an even more ancient writer, a priest—not quite of Rome—who had written both *Margery of Quether*, and *Onward Christian Soldiers*, the latter stirringly reminding us of the church militant against the powers of evil. Such encouragements Father Doyle drew from his sight of the abbey and the glories of her past. Yet his felt disquiet, uncertainty. If Tariq had been exorcised, it had not been by God's representatives, and indeed by a woman. And if he had not been exorcised? Was the enemy even now walking at his side? Had she saved his body to damn his soul?

"Tell me plain," he demanded when they had entered his house, where all the rooms had been blessed with holy water, "are you in league with the devil of hell or the good god?"

"Neither, though to us there is no *good* god or any *type* of god—Usen is one, goodness. Speak not the language of ancient polytheism, my learned friend—the better *translations* of your own book use it not for our age. And Usen we do not serve, but we worship him, and we serve humanity under his blessing. Yes, 'we', and we are not of humanity. You have been tested and have not been found wanting, except in lacking a little faith, my friend." He crossed himself, showing his fear. "We serve humanity, I said, fear not, believe only, and you shall see the true glory." All was silent for what seemed to be at least the space of half an hour. Cogitation time.

Finally Father Doyle broke the silence: "You are not human; you are not demonic; you are not angelic. Are you then not a spirit of deep heaven, of such as you spoke?"

"Yes, I am from Simboliniad."

"An evil spirit?"

"No, my friend, no longer, but once, once a dark queen", mused Lilith.

"As we returned, the abbey spoke to me of spiritual warfare—onward Christian soldiers. Are we not enemies at war?" asked Father Doyle.

"That song I know well. I also knew him who wrote it, who also collected what he believed were fairy stories—some were—one of which I played an unwritten part. Do you perchance recall the account written up by George Rosedhu who lived at Brinsabatch? Born in the C16, Margery of Quether had been a merry young wench. In church she had heard tell that eternal life could be had before death—true, but not the way she thought—and in her simplicity of mind had prayed for deathlessness. That was granted not by Usen, but by the vampires, and their gift became her curse.

"She had wandered long on lonely nights, begging for the endless life she thought to be a religious gift for the few, but had found it not. What she found was a vampire. Vampires often kill their meat, yet sometimes by slavery-bites—injection—they link their control to them, allowing them to walk this world in many forms."

"I have heard that story, though not told like that", said Father Doyle. "But did she not become a witch, evilly preying on mortals for her immortality?"

"Yes, hers was the sin even at the first, for though she understood not the preachment, she sought her own selfish vanity. And foolishly she wandered at night at a time when her people counselled—by way of caution—to forbear from crossing the moor in those dark hours when the powers of evil were exalted. Call her not *witch*, but rather a *corrumpi*, living for her vampire master as a slave. Not eternal life, but everlasting shadow was hers, a zone of existence between heaven and hell. I pitied her. I think that she still exists, sometimes waxing while those she drains wane—the life too often of my people. A dreary fate. Once she had a chance to be killed, but she would not believe her good fortune. A man named Solomon was all for burning her, misquoting the old line 'Thou shalt not suffer a witch to live'. Unwise was he, but alas for her that he slew her not in his folly." She sighed.

"Lilith, you tell me that the old line was misquoted, but I say to you that it was not", said Father Doyle heatedly.

"No, alas, misquoted it was. For do you not see that a time was when that small and narrow shepherd people had to be small and narrow—because they guarded a narrow way? For them witchcraft—many names speak of occult practices of evil—had to be dealt with sternly and swiftly, lest their unique voice was silenced. For that silence would have aborted the abundant life which was forming in their womb. But having played their part, their way has ended for their job was done—as it was it only narrowly succeeded. For your people the new and living way has come, in which rules made for former times no longer apply, though many rules made in former times still apply. For sometimes commands given them were global laws—like 'do not murder'. But some things were prophetic symbols—like 'do circumcision'—foreshadowings of greater significance, never needlessly imposed on other peoples but being Sinai specific, covenant ingredients for that meal, not for all meals. The horse that may not be ridden inside the stable is for riding outside. Solomon Davy counselled that witches should be burnt—not that he should be circumcised!—so misquoting, would have done self-righteous murder!"

"Then has the church been guilty of mass murder, frenzies of witch hunts?" asked Father Doyle in some unease.

"Yes of some, but mostly they were miscarriages of justice, and not as many as some rumours claimed. For around 400 years in your 'Middle Ages' it became something of a fashion, and an excuse for the cunning to steal from, or revenge upon, those whose lives or living they sought. On average some 100 died each year, some four women to every man. Maybe half were really executed for honest fear that they were witches.

But your people lacked understanding of the covenants within their holy book, so quoted laws long repealed by the Seventh Age.

Consider your Margery, of whom you have read. She was no witch, but her curse would at least have died with her ashes. I stood silently among the crowd alongside her namesake, daughter of Solomon. Yet I spoke to Margery without sound, showing her at least her way to partial deliverance—that way of giving back something of the *élan vital* she had leeched from Mr. Rosedhu—for her heart had rejected my promptings to find full deliverance through the flames. My friend, do you not see that I stand with humanity against the evil vampires, and that not all vampires are evil? Do you not see that, though not a Christian, as a soldier I fight alongside you in spiritual warfare?"

"Lilith, did not Father Cipolla speak truth when he said that the occult defiles our land, and that the blood of the occultists shall be upon their own heads?"

"He spoke some truth. Yes, they defile the land, but Usen permits them to live and to defile; he does not order that they be slain in carnal warfare. In his love he would shield them from evil, not slay them for evil. The sword was for a small place and for a short time—the wider way is now open and the sword is sheathed."

"You warned me of him. Tell me again, why?"

"Because his mind is in both light and darkness yet he knows it not, even as his tradition is in light and in darkness. He would counsel that all vampires should be slain. Are there not evil humans deserving of death, even as there are ethical humans deserving of life? He would slay the just with the unjust, all from the goodness of his heart and the blindness of his mind. He would slay me in his simplicity—if he could! Moreover, he would oppose the alliance of hobs, man, and sindeldi, in his inordinate fear of 'magic'. Yet there are troubles brewing for you and the other free peoples of this world, and I foresee that unless you unite you will fall separately and totally. You, my friend, have been granted a key to unite the foes of the true enemies. But you must be one at heart, undivided in conviction. It is for this that I have come alongside you."

"Why is it that Father Cipolla could not cast out these demons?"

"Though he relied too heavily on superstitions which were flung back in his face, the time was not right", replied Lilith.

"He told me that the Church worked no magic, and that Tariq had to play his part. How then can you say that he was too superstitious?" enquired Father Doyle.

"He spoke true when he said that the Church was not magic, but he did not base his own wisdom on that. Diaboloi flee before the command of faith, not by the objects of your faith. Water, crucifixes, these in themselves do not 'work'—though sometimes spirits play along to confuse you humans. Know you not of the seven sons of Sceva? If you focus your faith through objects, it is still your faith which they see projected through the objects, and that faith can move mountains. But sometimes the mountains have to be ready to being moved. He guessed aright that Tariq was not ready to let his mountain be moved—his life was built on that mountain howbeit on its cliff edge. Yet he saw not that the objects of faith were mere *objects* to the diaboloi which were not being ordered out by their host. Thus the objects commanded no respect. Thus he was puzzled, too used to exorcisms where the host is more ready to have their guests expelled by hook or by crook.

"As to our people, none but the weaker vampires were ever troubled by the crucifix, though the weak among you superstitiously swore by its purported power over us. Why should it have disturbed us, as if we, rather than the diaboloi, had been defeated by it? As for our weaker people, being of the Night it was a potent reminder of the Light, and as such could intimidate them who were weak unto death. To them only was it a holy terror that could chase them away—are there not some of you who flee from a ghastly noise or song? Indeed for some sufficient to snap their will that held body and soul together. As to the Light, although it was not us it had defeated, nevertheless we knew that one day the light would overcome the darkness in which we had become a part. For among us remained a dim yet potent prophecy of defeat."

"And you, Lilith, how did you succeed in exorcism, a woman and a Samaritan, so to speak?" asked Father Doyle more pacifically.

"By a simple word of command, for Tariq, having been brought to the hour of decision, was at last prepared to yield. Although not with the authority of your faith, nevertheless as a spirit of deep heaven my word carries weight. Indeed I am stronger than tertiary powers, and this they know, yet to cast them out before Tariq was ready would have been deadly to him, overthrowing his mind."

"While we raise such thing, can you tell me, why did Yahweh use the medium of Endor to rebuke King Saul, if *we* are not permitted to use the occult?" asked Father Doyle.

"My friend, your book—I love it well—speaks of Yahweh's sovereignty and man's sovereignty sometimes intending the same outcome from different motives. Both conspired to send Yosef to Egypt, but the former through love and the latter through hate. And when the time was ripe to move his people into Canaan, he used the double dealing pagan prophet Balaam, anointing him with the mind of the Ruach to divine the future. Pagan prophets were often misled—sometimes willingly—by the Necros, mere guessers of—and plotters for—the future. In fact that is why normally the chosen ones had to dispose of such magicians: it wasn't their false prophecies they feared, but their misunderstanding of true prophecy, persuasive misunderstanding because their own prophecies seemed so true.

"Did you not follow The Beast because it worked wonders? Balaam's blessings and cursings were matters of politics, policy-defining by the alleged authority of divinities. He was hired to curse in order to unite the opposition, warned to bless in order to disunite the opposition, and, trying to cash in the rewards of sin without death, openly blessed with his right hand yet with his left secretly suggested a policy to have them cut themselves off from those promised blessings. Poised between two worlds, unhappy Balaam had served two opposite masters, obeying what seemed like a foreign god by blessing the Chosen, and obeying mammon by suggesting the counter-policy of racial absorption. He was a clever and hapless man.

"The medium of Endor was like many a goodly woman, well-intentioned and caring, yet as weed planted among the prophetic field. The king, already disobedient, disobediently went to her and found himself in danger from a real visitation—the medium herself was scared by the unfamiliar familiar. The Samuel she 'brought up' wasn't the normal impersonation but the real deal, a one-off to show Saul that the disobedient can't even escape within the comfort of disobedience. The woman herself became a devout Yahwist after Saul's death, renouncing her Spiritualism.

"One of your lesser istari once commended the cleverness of spiritualists who baited their hook with ideas of literal family reunions 'on the further shore' pictured in entirely earthly terms, with ideas that things on the 'other side' are not so different after all, having the homely pleasures you wish in this life, the happy past restored. Yet Usen can use evil towards good ends unintended by evil. Yet beware, the occult is prone to deceive, and are you clever enough to direct it to the true good? You are not Usen. Let you mortals not dabble in it, for it will outmaster you. Tariq sold his soul and was torn, but now he is delivered and we should hear his story."

Knock, knock. At the door stood Tariq and Wilma, hand in hand, bashful. Wilma looked a little awed at seeing Lilith, but Tariq slightly bowed his head as if her presence was at least half expected. "Father, will you bless our marriage?" he asked.

"You wish me to marry you?" enquired Father Doyle.

"That would be no marriage," chuckled Tariq, "and I believe it is the spiritual custom that the man and the woman marry *each other*—true consent makes the marriage; we two are the *testigo*. It is your communal blessing we seek."

Father Doyle was thrown by that, and bumbled along in some confusion. "Wilma, I know, is water baptised, but what about you, Tariq? A sacramental marriage requires both to have gone through the sacramental door of water baptism, since that alone opens up all the sacraments."

"Your rhantism is not for me, Father, though I am now a believer", responded Tariq, looking enquiringly to Lilith.

"Tariq is one of ours, my friend, one from deep heaven and now a Hamashiachi as I. We do not go your ways, but respect those who sincerely do", said Lilith.

"Holy Mother of God, are we infested by powers beyond our ken?" stammered Father Doyle. "This I cannot take in in a moment. In this aftermath of war I have no bishop to call on, for we are all cut off by impassable roads and dangerous sea, even if I knew where a bishop lived. In such times I as priest must seek for myself the will of the Church. But, you Tariq, you are telling me that you are not even human, and wish to marry a daughter of Eve?"

"No Father, I am telling you that I am not human and *have* married this woman as we walked here to thank you", smiled Tariq. "We seek your blessing as the *de jure* spiritual leader of Whitby. Besides, my wife is Catholic." Looking upwards, Father Doyle breathed "Holy Mother, show me what to do."

"Perhaps I should tell you all my story, for when I proposed I merely told Wilma that I was now free to marry her, was a creature from beyond her kith and kin, had no wife, and would die soon", said Tariq softly.

"Merely?" muttered Father Doyle under his breath. He felt faint.

"Go on", said Lilith quietly.

"Yes my queen, for so still I hold you to be", said Tariq.

He gazed into Lilith's eyes and she returned his gaze. In telepathic link their minds flickered over the six Ages that were gone. They moved not nor spoke with mouth, and only their shining eyes stirred and kindled as their thoughts went to and fro, data transference far beyond the speed of lip. For the spirits of deep heaven need no fleshly bodies to speak, or air to carry their words, but can weave in and out in the spiritual dimension. Much could be compressed in short time.

After some few minutes he withdrew his gaze, and nodded. "Yes, I see that the story of our world has been told to you, Father. To you, wife Wilma, I say that she and I have existed since the dawn of time, created by the good will of Usen, and once lived as orbs of will within another galaxy. Our world perished, and we soon came to your world, drawn like moths by a sense that your world was to be the pivotal light of the universe. Yet here we found that we must weaken and were forbidden to depart. We became limited to mortal form—her majesty has I know said more—and became hunters needing prey.

"Too easily we turned to human blood—some still dread the vampire. Our own lives we led, yet not without order. Rules we made and rules we lived under, enrobing ourselves in shadow and secrecy. Some few who rejected the Night were shunned—at times they would be met and fought where no human witnessed our duals. My own darkness darkened. Seldom were we killed at first, in the days of our second strength, but as time rolled by we slowly weakened and became more vulnerable, for our wills no longer fully shielded our bodies. A very few have even died of frailty alone. I feared that I too should, and so that thrice I made an accursed pact to become a host, ever deeper bound.

"For we were not alone on what has become the silent planet. The Bent One, the once mightiest spirit under Usen, now lies trapped within its orb, commanding still a horde of lesser spirits who have always followed in his wake. These are totally evil, beyond repentance, beyond love. His toothless tertiaries are of lesser strength than we, even a weakened one such as I, and my queen could outmatch a whole legion of diaboloi. Yet I was frail and slowly dying—worn out before my time by my evils—and they offered me a surfeit of life in exchange for my soul, at least for its company: more evil; more life. They would intermingle with me, a cooperation of life, bodily possession in exchange for bodily repair. If ever a body was ruled by a cooperative it was mine. They thirsted for blood, not from deficiency but for delight, while I, having a mortal body, sought it for dependency.

"Alas, as a wolf pack we sought our quarry, and stirred up battles. After the Great Birth, a dunamos possessed me. Cruel as I was I sought but the fewest deaths, as Lilith is my witness; cruel as my guests were they sought the most deaths, as she well knows. It was easy for me as a bat between two sides, resting harmlessly on the pavilion of one army, then of the other, able as a man to enter the camps of both as a traitor selling the other's battle plans, trying to slightly unbalance both sides to gain the most deaths. My guests offered me fields of blood in which to drink my plot of blood to heart's ease. So what if I gorged myself? The mortally wounded would die anyway. Many a man over whom the battle had ridden, alone and dying felt my fangs and breathed his last. Now my fangs shall bite no more, for I shall not drink again until I drink from the blessèd cup of death and go to dwell with the unfallen.

"Such rivers of blood I had created, tormented by my inner diaboloi. Yes, even while I recently held honoured rank in the service of Brigantia, a Judas I became. My guests tired of long peace, and under their sway I came between King Venutius and his loving wife Cartimandua—though men joked that he was only king when under her and women tittered. Disquiet I sowed, and distrust; those who were joined I see I put asunder in envy, for their married bliss pained me. To both I carried false rumours of infidelity, of he with a Brigantian princess, of her with the Roman governor Ostorius Scapula. Neither were unfaithful, yet both soon lacked faith in the other, vexing them with baseless suspicions.

"Able to flit from place to place as a bat unmarked and then don human guise, I alone had created such dissention. Indignant the savage queen scandalously cast him off, and half in spite married another—some said a curse had been laid on the betrayer of Caratacus. The king then turned to vengeance upon her, dividing Brigantia and eventually bringing his former friend, Rome, into his bickerings and struggles for dominance—Rome too we had encouraged him to distrust. Thus through the quarrelling of two fools we had engineered a bloody chaos of war on which we feasted.

"Yet like a fool I rode with some few who fled to Wincobank from Stanwick, where in skirmish I was speared through the heart by a mean warrior, one I had carelessly mistaken for a corpse among the slain, a petty rider curled between the hoofs of his horse. A curse on Gnaeus Julius Agricola, Cur of Cerialis! And there unaided I should have died but for my guests and one new—for which favour they held me in compounded debt. For by their will I pulled forth the spear, and by their power my heart was reformed and my body healed. But they had grasped me the tighter in the saving. Small thanks had they from me, who many times had wished to have died. Damned fools they; doomed wretch I.

"Many places in this land I have indwelt, yet for millennia—flickers in time—I have abided in this shire. Many things of renown I have seen, some to the glory of Usen. One touched this town and my heart, for one of our nobles—though no longer in obedience—was ferried here by a ghost ship, from which he fled ashore as a demented dog. I sensed his nearness and soon heard his story. In his later years he had hidden within the ruling class, who gained liking for his stratagems against Turkey Land, but loathed him for his sadism expressed through a slave-son. Feigning death he resurfaced as a minor heir and took to something of the solitary life—I sensed that he kept somewhat from me. Pneumata can blend in among Psuchai in many ways. We can relocate, keeping our shape where none have seen us. We can extend our family lines by disappearing from one generation only to appear as a younger, though new moulds—generational reshaping—saps our dissipating strength. We can first live alongside a slave-heir, until donning their place and shape.

"Yet each new human shape we have to perfect for public display weakens us, and he was reaching the grave stage when intolerance to daylight becomes fatal. Being a recluse has its advantage, for by solitude his human shape could be kept unchanged, conserving and rebuilding his strength as a creature chained to nightlife, still slowly losing his remaining tolerance for daylight—perhaps this determined his downfall. Seeking fresh hunting grounds—or as I suspect to escape his jailers—he soon took ship to this island, but here, momentarily checked, he fled back until his new enemies had died.

"I heard later that they had pursued him and that by their hands he had died. I heard later that one of ours, Countess Dolingen, had pursued him, and unseen had helped the human hunters take their prey by binding him through his fear of Lilith. They knew it not. It was with amaze that I read in their journals that they had believed that he must die for their sakes and for his—that they had loved him as themselves. We sneer at their foolish belief that vampires themselves are possessed humans eternally damned unless released from their possessed bodies. Can only dogs possess dogs? The possessors are vampires; the possessed are human. Such fools could not save him and he perished in his sins, his body burning to ashes as the light he had cursed fast bound him as he lost heart and head to the knife. Yet their naive goodness in trying to help their enemy, spoke to us who had deemed them but puerile prey.

"My own sins over bitter millennia were no less, and I deserved no better fate and have known bitterness of soul and weariness of mind. In my brief time here the Henges of Thornborough I have seen raised. Some entombed there had yielded to me their life's blood. Spears and arrows of flint were then as now the weapons of death. Over the mortal millennia, some of my kind have been slain here: the bodies of those of the water-clan were sealed in barrows, their spirits linger still in slow decaying undeath. Their kind I pity most; the fire-clan speedily depart, the ice-clan can return, but the water-clan cling on without mortal hope. And at Upton Hill a lady, guised as a Saxon princess, long seemingly lay asleep on her barrow bed. To me she was 'Zara'. She I mourned, for she I loved.

"Yes, even possessed, some remnant of creaturely love—which is denied in the Dark—has held my cruelty in check and my will in division. I have oft visited my folk as they dwell yet in their barrows, but now they only gibber—I cannot now talk with them, feeble ghosts still resisting their watery fate to dwell in true shadow.

"I await the prophecy of Ragnarok, foretold in ancient times, but I think I shall not live to see it. For thus spoke Laleocen, mad seer of Coed Celyddon: 'Alas, thou walkest sadly the earth and rideth upon the heavens as neither a quick nor a dead. Alas ancient of days wearied beyond count of days. Thy body thou holdest tight in thine hands, yet it is but a body of undeath. In a time to come thou must look beyond the waters towards the sun's set, yielding up thy death to live beyond thy body. But long thou shalt wander enslaved, thinking that thou art free, yet in surrender alone is freedom. One of thy own shalt beyond hope offer thee the freedom thou cravest. Seek, and thou shalt find, if thou wilt but open both thy hands to release thy death, and then thou shalt play thy part in the restoration, though thy body shalt not endure the yellow dragon.' These words I have long pondered, telling me of my death from undeath. I shall depart west over water. My wife shall mourn for me, and rejoice."

All sat quietly. The morning had worn on and Father Doyle and Wilma drew aside for devotions, while Tariq and Lilith communed in silence. Both seemed to sense something brewing in the wind. After that the humans broke their fast. Lilith's hunger could not be met from Father Doyle's pantry, and Tariq would drink no more until he found the true kingdom beyond the confines of the west.

∞

But with that same dawning of the sun a group of hunters, led by Bram the head hunter, awoke from their bivouac at Briggswath by Esk. Some village dwellings remained, and though mainly roofless offered protection from the elements. Curiously there were numerous bats hanging around under such roofing as remained, chattering away nineteen to the dozen. The human hunters were not afraid of their little black friends!

Still remembered in awe were two hunters, Lif and his wife Lifthrasir, who had arrived upon the wings of a storm from northern lands of merciless ice and brooding mountains. Tough they were, resilient, seers and storytellers both. They whispered of man's rebirth yet to be, spoke in riddles of visions of dark spirits awakening from slumber as giants of nature, of a fell wolf bound fast in chains, of the darkening of the sun. They always hunted alone together. Strangely, they had feared bats, and many had chuckled. They had inspired confidence, but now they were gone, seeking their northern shores. It was their destiny, they had said.

But bats were harmless. As normal, two guards had kept watch, dividing their shifts into three or four watches. They were getting to know the lay of the land. Typically hunters carried hand-sized chunks of graphite in animal pouches, and animal hides on which they could chart their journey. For besides fresh game and flint, the survivors at Whitby needed to know what the surrounding land was like, and still hoped to find pockets of people with whom they could connect.

At traces of old human habitation they briefly searched for old place names and jotted some down: it is easier to say "rendezvous in Houlsyke" than to say "meet you about 15 kilometres west of Whitby" and besides, they craved a sense of their pre-apocalyptic past. At the instigation of Father Doyle a map house had been set up to collate data from these forays—the walls became maps, North, West, South—indicating safe places, the terrain, and what the land offered. Townsfolk regularly spent time there memorising the lay of the land, for one never knew whether a crisis would lead to abandoning the safe haven of Whitby. The Beast might yet decide to mop up human stragglers by sending in sandbots—hopefully never by the overkill of radiation.

Father Doyle regularly taught reading and writing, having been a studious student in Redcar Shelter where power had allowed the Roman Files to run—Ainet had permitted humanities to be stored, but science and mathematics had been officially lost. Each hunting party was able to take at least someone with basic read/write skills.

Bram's team had been hunting and scouting as far as the Esklets near Westerdale, a route that had proved fairly safe. A brisk six hour walk on a pleasant day without a care in the world, would have taken them there. But when potentially in enemy territory, where ambuscade by mutant animals was a constant fear, hiding rather than hygge was their mindset, and stealth-mode the name of the game. They walked slowly, cautiously, and allowed a full week for their reconnaissance. A lot of stopping, lying low, listening—the howlers were always best avoided—scenting the air, crawling, cautious walking interspersed with quick dashes though open fields—but life was worth it. It was dangerous, and the hunters were wary, at nights setting fires for defence yet shielding their light from creatures of the night. They washed themselves in the Esk, and then rubbed on mud to reduce their scent.

And it had gone well. The other day they had shot some game, added mud to the arrow wounds, and stored the bodies into sacks. Rabbits, rats, fawns—the mutant varieties anyway. All seemed well, when out of the blue two howlers sprung at them from cover. Alwin and Gilbert, caught unawares and off guard, were thrown to the ground, and the howlers slashed their throats. But then the hunters—now the hunted—brought their weapons to bear. Arrows were fired into the howlers. That infuriated them. But howlers can take many arrows without real hurt.

They rushed at the group. Galfrid's spear was thrust aside and he went down with a howler at his throat. Edmund kicked the howler's head, only to have his offending leg badly ripped. Dauid lunged a spear into the howler, which grabbed the spear before dispatching Galfrid. Dauid released that spear, and stabbed with another. This time the howler sprung away, ripping out the first spear and snapping it as a twig. It glared at its attacker. By its size a female, perhaps, though many howlers had hair like great apes making it difficult to judge the sex. No doubt the males could—even lower beasts could always tell between males & females!

Then it charged straight into his spear, its arms extended to grab its prey. As luck would have it—if luck there be—Dauid's spear butt was pressed to a rock. The howler's own rage impaled it, and it stood transfixed, howling, its misshapen teeth inches from Dauid's face, its hand around his neck to tear. Bram attacked from the rear, forcing it back along the spear shaft.

The other howler bludgeoned Cutbert to death, whose spear thrust had merely grazed the creature. Randulf and Roger both ran at it, their spears wounding chest and thigh. It pushed forward, causing them to stubble. Roger never arose, the creature spearing him with his own bloody spear. The other it flung away in rage, pulling up Randulf to its feebly bleeding chest for a fatal embrace. Alan and Edmund fired arrows into its back and neck. Tossing Randulf to the ground it turned its attack against them. Alan was throttled, but Edmund swept up a rock and stuck hard upon the howler's head. Something cracked, and it stood dazed, never releasing its grip as Alan's body drooped insensate. Slowly, a low growl in its throat, it released the body, then staggered back and sank to the ground. Edmund struck again and it lost consciousness.

Its wounded mate, if mate it was, glared at the living men—Bram, Dauid, Edmund, and Randulf. It attacked again. This time all four speared it from four directions, holding it transfixed, impotent. Pressing home and twisting their points, with a final howl it slowly died, still snapping its teeth. Bram and Edmund alone unscathed, ensured that the other would rise no more, while Randulf attended to Dauid's badly bleeding neck.

The sub-intelligent howlers had never been known to silently approach and lie in ambush, and this intelligent tactic was an immediate cause for concern, as was the smell of blood which would attract other mutants. No longer were the meat sacks a cause for thanksgiving, and they were promptly emptied and the sacks tied empty around them. They hastened to the river, quickly washed their wounds, and rapidly returned to Whitby keeping close to the Esk, spurning the remains of old roads, for a river still afforded some protection by swimming if attacked: howlers would probably jump in and be drowned—their human minds seldom seemed to caution them. Survival spurred their flight.

All were badly scratched by the brambles they thrust through. At Ruswarp Dauid, still bleeding badly, bled no more. His body was lowered into the river, for it was feared that one bloodied by a howler could return from death to join their ranks. What was sense, and what was superstition? Playing on the side of superstition seemed to make best sense.

Thus it was that of ten sent out, only three returned to tell their tale of woe and horror. And thus it was that a pounding on Father Doyle's door revealed three agitated hunters just returned, bloodied and exhausted. Not standing on ceremony, they immediately informed Father Doyle of the terrible attack within that last hour. "Father," said Bram, the head hunter, "last night we camped only a few cautious hours from the perimeter, for it had gotten too dark to travel safely. We rose with the sun, and had started on our way back when we were attacked. Most of us were butchered. But Father, it was a silent ambush by howlers."

"The self-same hour I cast out diaboloi", said Lilith. "If they have discovered a new type of host, they could command an army of howlers. Vampires hunt howlers for blood, and they who fear no other fear us. But if the diaboloi have found new compatibility, their cunning will be added to the howlers, making them useful weapons of war against mankind."

Tariq spoke up: "I fear that I have brought the evil ones into this town, and that unleashed they will now focus their attack here in their fury.

My queen, you and I could stand against them, but could we protect the humans?" He looked protectively towards Wilma.

"We could not protect all. Boats could remove some to the safety of the sea, but howlers possessed are a new threat that might not die overnight. Tariq, my friend, your time has come to play your part." Bram, Edmund, and Randulf, looked on in wonderment. Lilith they knew to be a herbal healer, and Tariq a moody man not to be crossed. Why they were there, and why Wilma was there, they did not understand. Had they interrupted some kind of exorcism or aftermath?

"My friends all, Tariq must fly to the Isle of Woods to raise the sindeldi. The power of the diaboloi is not to increase the howlers, but to control those already bred. We must burn that hand of control, for they must leave these mutants of man to their miserable fate. Their numbers in these parts are low, and it will take time to summon more, yet within days there could be an army, and dark vampires are gathering. Tariq can warn the hobs of this new threat, and travel swiftly to the island and back. I shall remain here, guarding this town and its people." With Father Doyle's assent she said, "Tariq, do quickly what you must do, but this hour I give you."

"Yes, my queen." He departed with Wilma—blessed by the sign of the cross—to her old home down the street, yet by noon he would be gone.

Refreshed, Tariq tenderly kissed his new bride. Never had he broken faith with a woman; never would he do so—he was not a man that he should lie and what he said, he would do. Contented within Usen he knew that whatever his fate, she should have fruit. Opening the bedroom window he fluttered once or twice outside, then off over the bay. "At this time of day?" ejaculated a weathered fisherman, "bats at this time of day? Whatever next, that's what I want to know." Even Lilith wondered, for little did any know what the prophetic clock would bring. Intentional prophecy was just that, a declaration of intent, provisional. An intended blessing could be called off if the good it was to bless, became bad; an intended cursing could be called off if the bad it was to curse, became good. Interactive, is the word.

Does prophecy die by a thousand qualifications, or does it live as we do who speak intention obviously open to change in the light of changes? Determinism is a damnable doctrine if taken too far. There were many *ifs* in Tariq's mission, and no one should ever sit back and thoughtlessly let a personal prophecy do its own thing as if magic— they are interactive and intentional of divine intervention. It may well be that Usen had a contingency plan covering a Here Am I, Send Aaron, but Tariq had no intention of weaselling out of the prophecy. In shape a mere microbat, yet in speed surpassing Thor the Thunderer himself, he sped speedily through the air. In Runswick Bay Sarad, having smoked his pipe, was just about to return to his hole where his table was all laid out and a rabbit stew with taters and carrots was simmering over his hearth.

"Greetings Sarad", said Tariq. Sarad jumped and spun around.

"Now who the dickens are you and how did you get here?" asked Sarad.

"I, Tariq of Whitby, am come from Lilith and Father Doyle bearing tidings of great woe. Yet there is hope. My story is short: diaboloi have possessed the howlers of the night, imbuing them with endurance of the light and cunning beyond their kind, adding to their woes. Now the town is endangered indeed, and I fear that greater jeopardy is to come unless the enemy is soon checked. I seek out Ránpalan the hidden king. An alliance must be formed between the free peoples of Middle-earth."

Sarad bowed low—"Welcome. I was just about to eat. Would you care to join me? But, please don't think me rude, how *did* you get here?"

"I am vampire, but fear not, I hold Lilith to be my queen, and we are Hamashiachim", replied Tariq. "Eat if you will, I will not, but talk I will and listen you must." Somewhat apprehensively the old hob was bustled into his hole, musing that it might be provident that Bella and their children had not returned. It was all very well to dismiss Father Cipolla's bigotry against the vampires, but meeting one face to face, actually leading one of them into your hole, privately tested your public belief that they were not all evil. "If I perish I perish, and that's all there is to it," thought Sarad, "but if he's as he says he is—and he used the holy name, like—well then this could be a turn up for the dark side. But what does he want of me, aye we wonders."

Very soon his fears were relieved as Tariq, who had picked up from Lilith the gist of Father Doyle's encounter with the hob, proved by his knowledge that he was a trusted ambassador. Fortunately it never crossed Sarad's mind that Tariq could have eavesdropped as a shape-shifter. But anyway, Tariq spoke with the ring of truth. "Well, Mr. Tariq, your news is disconcerting, definitely disconcerting, yet your mission is of hope. Yes, hobs will help in your quest. I wish now that my Bella my missus was here to hear this. She's gone with a party of hobs to our holes over Baysdale way, just past the old Haggaback Farm and agin the Hograh Moor, just below Gin Garth of Black Sike. A safer place you couldn't wish to find, and all snug and dry within. A number of hobbets and hobbins have gone there."

The upshot was that Sarad gave Tariq names, locations, and passwords of hobs living in Porthmadog, who in turn knew hobs living in Ballymoney over Water, who would in turn put Tariq in touch with other hob communities. In turn each would send out scouts to look for Ránpalan the hidden king, and would also seek for a working alliance with the big people. By the power of his will Tariq could then fly from community to community almost in the bat of an eye, picking up any information unearthed as to Ránpalan's whereabouts, though he had a hunch that if his old friend heard who sought him, then he would be able to let him know telepathically the instant that he was found. His own telepathy was severely limited, but Ránpalan's? Tariq left Sarad to his stew and flew straight to Porthmadog, and from there to Ballymoney.

On their own turf, hobs weren't generally difficult to spot for the eagle-eyed flyer, and of the water-clan he had had no problem crossing the watery divide. Once upon a time man had had flying machines, and in those days hobs had been as canny about concealment from the air, as from the land and sea. Hobs had relaxed their guard in daylight hours. Besides, they knew that vampires were night flyers. Well, they simply didn't expect one espying them from the sunny heights, and it was disturbing when Tariq had landed among them. But with the passwords given and his mission uncovered, they happily fell in with the plan. Thus it was that before the night had fallen, several hob communities were already sending scouts to look for the hidden sindeldi.

The Isle of Woods! Much could be said about its dreamy past. Long long before this time of apocalypse and post-apocalypse, that most ancient of races—the slow-moving tree shepherds—had become divided, wives and daughters sundered from husbands and sons. Who is to say how they were sundered without trace? Perhaps the sea covered the tracks of the seekers of spring and summer. Long in the east the fruit bearers had put down roots, garden roots that were torn up by their dark enemy, the Evil Eye that had infested the land and hated it flora. They escaped south, then somewhat north and westward. Long they had been lost to their husbands and sons until sindeldi seeking a new home had found them, which in turn led to a migration of the pollen bearers from their old forests to re-join them.

Many songs had been sung of that great search which had only ended in the autumn of their lives within Middle-earth. Much their reunion had enriched the trees of the isle, giving it its name of the Isle of Woods. Yet finally the winter of their time in Middle-earth came, and they followed the call from the Powers of the West, to take sail over water, and thence over the water bridge, to the true land of willows beyond Middle-earth. Thus united had they left Middle-earth, having established an island paradise of woods. And thus it was that many hobs, humans, and sindeldi, had moved to that isle, of beauty green unsurpassed. And thus it was that Tariq rested briefly in within the beauty of fair Crookedwood.

The next day more and more communities had been located and had joined the search, and late morning hobs from Poulaphouca had made contact with a sindeldi patrol around Ballysmuttan. Guarding the perimeter of the sindeldi stronghold, Belegon had surrounded the hobs unawares—the sindeldi are stealthier than even hobs and can even hear them breathing at a distance.

But sindeldi are kindly folk and do not kill without good reason. For their part the hobs had not been stealthy but had been calling out as they briskly journeyed, that they sought Ránpalan, for otherwise they might have been allowed to pass unawares, as both man and hobs had often done.

Under caution, Leath, himself an elf-friend, had told how Brogan his village chief (and its shoemaker for the big people whom they aided) had sent out search parties at the request of Tariq of the vampires, who wished to meet his old friend Ránpalan to their mutual advantage. He quickly added to the incredulous sindel that Tariq—a name once feared as evil—had become a shadowminder.

As is commonly known, sindeldi are not normally friends with vampires, even the good kind. Belegon nevertheless had promised to send back the message. The hobs, led by Leath, had been warned that they must venture no further until the king's will was known: some waited there and some returned to their holes. So it was that Tariq soon after noon presented himself at Ballysmuttan, and was placed under close guard by Belegon. Before the second day ended all the hobs had returned to their village, and Tariq had been taken blindfolded through one of the hidden doors into Ránpalan and Queen Kemeniel's underground kingdom.

"Hail, king, may the stars ever shine upon your face, and yours, O Lady fair, beloved of the king", said Tariq bowing low.

"You are welcome, Tariq, for well do I recall your timely help when I with scouts was exploring Brigantia. But for your aid the sheorcs would have surely slain us, I deem. I marvelled then that one of the vampires, one who lived on human blood, would protect sindeldi."

"In those days my mind was in two, O King. We had in the most descended into selfish wickedness, becoming haters of the light. However some were still haunted by the light of deep heaven from which we had come to your world. Never has dunamos or tertiary of the Necros turned, but vampires have—even my queen, Lilith, thanks be to Pantocrator. My mind is now one and the time of my departure is near. I call now for an alliance of light against the alliance of darkness which I fear is forming." Tariq waived away refreshments that were being offered to him: "I no longer drink except the one blessed drink of good death into which I shall soon be baptised."

"Truly" said Kemeniel, "a good death in a blessing beyond price—are you prepared?" She with a spirit of prophecy foresaw his death and his new temptation not to die.

"Yes," said Tariq, "my heart is set my lady."

"What then is this dark alliance of which you speak?" asked the king.

"My lord king, I have of late dwelt with humans in a small port that faces east towards Sjaelland, remnants from the attack by that they called Ainet, and now simply The Beast. Separated from my own kind, long have I forgone food. Many an acorn has become a mature tree since I last drank, though tormented for blood. For I have been enslaved by the diaboloi."

"Tariq, know you not that that accursèd people are rebels incorrigible? How came you who spared my life, to dwell in company with the damned?"

"To live, my lord, yet bondage to them was a living death to me, which I despised. Even my prior sins I despise. Many are the traditions and superstitions that arose within humanity against us. But of all the calumny set to our door, the worst at least was false, which was that we could eternally damn souls whom we had enslaved. Befogged by this folly, some earnestly believed that they needed to sever heads and hearts so as to return the enslaved to humankind for the chance of heaven— little did they understand the soul. Even some of *us* suffered that fate by benign humans believing that we were humans under Necuratu! My Carpathian friend suffered that very fate, and his dying bemusement was misread as peace.

"Yet they were right to sever us will from body, for we were man killers and enslavers, disgracers of the Imago, and once severed could neither kill nor curse no more. And right too to destroy the undead bodies of their own kind, blessedly releasing sooner than would otherwise have been, the enslaved into the welcome arms of death, whichever fate awaited them.

"Alas for such like old Margery. For the enslaved were cursed with undying slavery by our gift of thelodynamics, a gift commuted by death. So perhaps the superstitious fools were not so foolish after all, though slandering us as more powerful and demonic than we were, 'evolving' they said 'in evil'. Usen himself they misjudged as eternally damming the slaves for the sins of their masters—can he not divide soul from soul at the resurrection?

"I as a slaver was myself enslaved by my sin. Only of late have I been freed by my queen. Never was she a thrall of diaboloi, nor dwelt with them, yet was more evil than I. Yet by the grace beyond deep heaven she has longer been freed, and been to the secondborn a shadowminder. But know, O King, that I have these many weeks heard the howls of my kind—the howls of The Forming in bloodlust—and the howls of howlers, those misshapen of mortal man, who howl but in anguish. The Forming is a coming together in strength, which I fear forebodes none other than the preparation of war against man. Moreover the dunamoi of darkness are among the vampires but not to harm. Is this not alliance?

"Only days ago the diaboloi have moved to possess the howlers. That too is new and worrying. The howlers are prey to vampires, unappetising but useful blood-givers, but their minds are zombified, of little use to any. But as fighters the threshold of their pain is without peer. The diaboloi could use them as drone fighters, and alongside the vampires they would form a terrible alliance against man. And if man falls, such an alliance could search out hobs and sindeldi singly, and destroy them singly. Vampires of the Light there are that would help, but we as would fight for the free peoples are too few against our fallen brethren."

"Tariq, why should such alliance form at this time? Never before have your kind sought such an alliance with the demon kind, nor they with you", Ránpalan enquired.

"I do not know", replied Tariq. "Indeed I hoped that maybe you O King might have seen the answer."

"Tariq, your words say more than they seem. Speak, what mean you by 'seen the answer'?" demanded the king.

With a hidden smile Tariq replied: "Long before the pyramids of Egypt I heard rumour of the seeing stones of the First Age. Long did I search, with many clues pointing to the king of the sindeldi. Indeed, but for the sheorcs I might have ransacked your camp in secret search—but I could not let them slay you in their bloodlust so rescued your camp instead, lesser evil defeating greater evil. Was it not in Usen's will that that night of all nights was the one in which I stole into your camp with theft in mind, that same night the sheorc horde strove to overcome?"

"Praised be the pantocrator, the sovereign of sovereigns", sighed Kemeniel in love.

Ránpalan was no fool. Long had he wondered whether the coincidence of the camp had been a diabolical plot to lull him into false trust. Yet Tariq felt as one who walked in the light of the pantocrator, and Kemeniel saw deeply into hearts.

Spake Ránpalan: "It is true, though a thing hidden, that here in my kingdom is the seeing stone of hands. So the eyes of Mullaghcleevaun are not blind, but the stone of seeing no longer looks to Middle-earth. For know you that the stones of seeing are not magic. Though their flesh is of substance from the earth, yet into each a Power entered willingly as to a world of surpassing crystal beauty. They were thus homes beautifully crafted, in which sizeless Powers could dwell alone.

"On earth there are creatures of flesh that also create and enter into shells, both on the land and in the sea. In exchange these Powers, whose vision ranged the earth, could reveal to those who held the stones what it was they saw, or what the seeker sought to see. They could even speak with the voice of the seeker to another stone handler. Yet the handler could afflict the indweller, and the stone of hands once suffered terribly from the fate of a handler who died holding it in horror, marring it. In mercy I perceived its pain, and in mercy released its gaze from Middle-earth. It now looks to deep heaven, to the kingdom of Asgard, and finds solace. Thus to Middle-earth I am blind, save for the birds that tell me news and scouts that seldom range far. A wanderer to and fro I am no longer, and gather now moss not news.

"It was indeed no doubt intended that you came with evil intent that night, when worse came with worse evil intended. And it is no doubt intended that you should come thus to me again—for my heart speaks clearly to me. At this conjunction in time, one of the vampires newly redeemed comes from Lilith—whose story we know—and warns of an alliance of disjointed evils. I must put away all doubts and doubt not that this is a clarion call to arms. The hidden kingdom must come forth. Yet we are diminished, even if all sindeldi who went not into the true west were brought together.

"Perhaps it is not so strange that your thoughts have been on the seeing stone. Assuredly the pantocrator has spoken now with your voice. Herein is salvation, I deem. For know you that in Asgard there dwells another stone of seeing, of beauty like to the moon in her fullness. A powerful stone once held by the enemy himself, and after him buried deep in molten lava. Dwarves of Nidavellir found it and treasured it, until losing it in a contest of wisdom to Odin, Allfather to his people. Righty was it renamed the Eye of Odin. Asgard has along with all Kingdom Powers been severed from the realm of man, yet it is said that they of Asgard have yet a part to play. The Eye of Odin now ever looks to Midgard, which we call Middle-earth. I shall speak to King Odin, for this may be his Ragnarok Day." With that the king departed into his inner chambers where the stone of hands lay hidden deep.

Hidden deep within his lair in Wraithwaite, Pazuzu had sensed the flight of Tariq overhead, and pondered what that might mean. Tariq had been an increasingly reluctant ally, but against the powerful shadowminder Lilith, had been a welcome one. Now the diaboloi's control over him had been broken, which in turn strengthened the hand of Lilith. But yesterday had also been the day that the fleeing tertiaries had accidentally discovered that the local howlers could, though with some difficulty, be controlled, a control satisfactorily tested against some human hunters. Thus a potential new weapon against the human vermin was on tap. Moreover, vampires had recently realised that their survival required a complete takeover of humanity. Pazuzu was a dunamos with legions of tertiary diaboloi under his command, but controlling humanity without vampire support was problematic. Humans could resist the dark power to death or to insanity, but his people did not wish them deceased or deranged, for a global threat was rearing its head, a threat which could make this world dead to them.

His kind actually needed creatures of flesh and blood for their sport, even meeting some need for companionship, a need never to be publicly admitted. Isolation was not so glorious in the Necros, and reigning in hell was reigning alone. Naturally the zombified were of no real interest to them. Minds marred into the subhuman mattered little—it was the Images of Usen that they enjoyed tormenting, an oblique way of getting back at Usen himself, and offering some form of diabolical satisfaction. Even the Mashiach had gotten into the game and been soundly beaten—soundly whipped, he would never do that again! Every dunamos could lick its cracked lips and taste that recent triumph, truly a high point in history.

Regarding the vampires, they were not easy to possess, and indeed were not of this world so were not generally the game of diaboloi, but at least they could be strong allies. Over weeks they had been amassing in the vicinity, and now their queen, Rangda, who shared his taste in blood, had come to him to confer. Moving expeditiously could take advantage of Tariq's removal—a window of opportunity had been opened.

Pazuzu smiled indulgently upon the queen of the Night as if his queen, but only as a king in chess smiles upon his queen—she is strong, sacrificable, but not spellbinding. He had dealt with her kind once before, when a vampire prince from the Carpathian Mountains had landed at Whitby—dog eat dog. Human pilgrims long visited Whitby, just as Catholics had visited the bones of Santa Claus in the Italian town of Bari. Hoaxing humanity was hilarious.

"Rangda, dost thou understand that the humans have to be dominated, and that we must forget former disagreements?" Pazuzu sat before her not as a shadow of despair but in his form of a lion-headed man, with wings folded behind him.

"I do. Your people and mine had gone separate ways, seldom meeting in solidarity. Yet both hostile to humanity, you to disturb blood, we to drink it. There has been more than enough for us both, so we have not fought as antagonists, but now that the earth giant rears its head we must fight as allies. For behold, the yellow stone glows red, as you have in these last few weeks shown us. Man was the scientist—never to our interest—and managed to sap its strength—that was to the common good. But that power they so foolishly handed over to that they now call The Beast, which now has let slip that control—does it seek a barren world to itself, its very flora and fauna withered beyond recall? Unthinking mind! The yellow stone waxes, and soon the world shall darken under a sky of deep dark dust, and our prey shall be lost to us both. Then we too shall perish for want of blood, while your people shall but wither without the Great Game. And which shall be worse?"

"But of course ye need not perish, and we need not wither, for their chariots of fire can take us beyond the confines of this world, to new worlds to colonise, to control, to confuse. But we must first assimilate the creatures of the chariots into our will and our plan. Yet the key is with The Beast, so we must together overcome The Beast, and then with human hands unlock these ships of theirs, turning them to our purposes. That the diaboloi cannot do alone, and thy kind is skilled to absorb these creatures more easily than can we", said Pazuzu.

"Strange," said Rangda, "that our prey provides the escape for us both. Yes," said she stroking her protruding fangs with feminine pride, "the night kingdom will ally with the dark kingdom. For humans now must be more than our meat, and must be our means to depart this dying world, beyond the reach of the Cosmic Powers that have hemmed us in by the Eighth Law that forbids Powers and Pneumata, once within this world, to by their own power depart. By engineering and natural philosophy man has at last offered us a way—and given us the need—to fly into the heavens, escaping the confines of this world. And man we can release back into the Great Game, if by chance we find indeed a hospitable world."

Pazuzu chuckled: "Yea, a world perhaps unguarded, helpless before us. Many have been the Guardians to this world, Powers unfallen or Powers mixed, Powers now standing back within the spiritual, cut off from the carnal. Yet they added challenge to the game."

"A deadly game, O Dark Prince. Long did I fight against Guardian Barong, and took grievous harm before overcoming my enemy. Scars I still bear. Yet I revel in fight, and grieve his loss. Those we hate give zest to life, so victory entails loss. Is it not strange? Yet now we must flee or fall forever: what would you have us do?"

Pazuzu clicked his eagle-like talons together, and chuckled once more. Rising, he beat his hideous wings, and the air stunk. "We shall descend with inescapable force upon the enemy, not to slay but to bind. Thy kind shall absorb them into subjection. Then with hordes of howlers as our vanguard—they shall doubtless be cut to ribbons by the machines—vampires and humans shall follow unscathed in their wake. In this way we must overrun APOC and gain the secrets to their flying machines, rising thus to the chariots that encircle, and then escape from the Powers that have bound us here. But first we shall prise the prey from its stronghold of Whitby, defeat its shadowminder thereby disheartening all other shadowminders, and in the sweeping into the camps of the prey they shall hear the sound of inevitability—they shall be ours."

Thus it was that as the sun sank on the second day, Whitby was awakened by the noise of battle. In anticipation diaboloi had herded howlers from the shire and beyond, and howlers controlled by tertiaries threw themselves against the defences and defenders, north, west, and south. Their controllers had muzzled them as they silently approached the town, but once unleashed their wayward wantonness in battle could not be fully quelled—human life would inevitably be lost. Some howlers simply threw themselves onto the stakes picketing the town, skewered but still howling for blood.

Others tried scrambling up the walls, or threw themselves as battering rams against the gates.

Three gates there were. The Southgate bordering on the Abbey perimeter, where Abbey Lane led to Robin Hood's Bay coastal road; the Yorkgate, where Saint Hilda's road met the Stakesby road to York; the Northgate, where the Upgand road met the Staithes coastal road. The town had been downsized for better defence, yet still allowed for population growth. Buildings outside that perimeter had been cannibalised to build a surrounding wall and to repair buildings within. The land beyond had been kept clear of trees though some scrub had reclaimed the denuded land. Only some few buildings beyond had been kept in hope of one day being able to safely reoccupy. But homes that had not been wasted in long years past were not wasted in yielding help in the now. Nor wasted were the hours of sweat and toil of men, women, and children, in building the wall.

The town was secure; the guards raised the alarm. And the households of Whitby grabbed weapons stored close to their doors and went forth to fight. Father Doyle had with their leaders taught them that it was likely death to remain indoors if ever attacked. A solid front of defence was needed, and men, women, and even the children old enough to help the adults, had to fight to survive. They had trained against such a day.

Harpoons proved mighty weapons, but all too few, all too few. From the walls arrows and spears rained down on the howlers, and some, pierced by many a point, gibbered like screaming pin cushions still seeking to rip and to slay: like dead bodies, howlers were slow to discharge their putrid blood—they were slow to die.

The Bridge Watchers quickly smeared the bridge with oil, a former swing-bridge rebuilt in such a way as to burn quickly to defend either east or west if the west or east wall were breached. New Bridge, though outside of the town perimeter, had sadly proved too difficult to dismantle, thus affording enemies easier means to coordinate attacks from both sides of the Esk.

Pazuzu and Rangda had led a horde over to the high ground of the south. The vampires were less prominent in the fray, held back for the domination of the defeated, and to come against Lilith if she rose to the challenge. This she sensed but yet she came, and came in great wrath from the Southgate, the abbey to her side, her bright eyes burning like fire. None of the howlers would face her but fled, their very guests fearing her wrath uncloaked. And few of the vampires dared the encounter, boastful though they had been against their former queen. Some dared, their corpses short-lived monuments to their folly.

Rangda threw her will against Lilith. Dark violet light came from her outstretched arms, flinging the body of Lilith through the air. Yet at once she arose, a cold silver light stabbing through the night air, straight into the heart of Rangda, who in turn was flung far into the surrounding heather. Singed, she staggered to her feet. Never before had she met such might. Had the old queen been reborn?

As a mighty rushing wind Pazuzu descended from the night sky, twisting around to grapple with Lilith from behind, pinioning her arms to her sides, clawing into her flesh with his loathsome talons. Pazuzu, demon king of the south wind. She flexed her arms, light as power pulsated through her body, and Pazuzu's grip was broken like a twig. Rangda sprang upon her enemy at the same time as Pazuzu rebounded upon her. Gripped by both assailants, Lilith was hard pressed to remain upright. Pushing, twisting, she summoned her silvern power and again shook off her foes. Then shafts of silver flame again leapt forth from her hands, one into Pazuzu, the other into Rangda. This time Rangda felt the poison of Lilith battling with her very will. Sight failing her, nausea wracking her body, she stumbled away from the fray, leaving Pazuzu to abide Lilith alone.

Alone he hurled his crimson fire at her, yet this time Lilith caught it in a silver web of power. Foiled it flickered and was snuffed out. Then she silently took his eye and their wills blazed. Face to face they stood, the battle going on at a distance around them, the strength of their will pitted each against the other. Lion-headed he roared his vexation, unable to outmatch her, while she stood in glowing confidence, knowing that grace had been given her to more than match her diabolical foe, this prince of darkness. Steadily she stepped slowly towards him.

He quailed and stepped back, his wings outstretched in puffed up majesty. She smiled grimly, her hands illuminating with lunar light. Forward she moved and he, cowed and defeated at last, with uproarious wings rose aloft. Crimson fire rose to his hands, but Lilith's flames were suddenly around him, burning, eating into his frame, and with a cry of anguish he flew from her across the town, seeking what he may devour. Yet she, still bleeding from his claws, took to monstrous bat form and pursued her deadly foe, allowing him no rest to wreak his revenge upon mortal man.

Thus over the west cliff they flew, and thus he sped the town while she engaged the howlers who contested the North Gate by the White House. Their generals had deserted them, and the will that had driven them to madness turned to mayhem. The howlers fled from the field of battle, and the vampires fled before them dismayed by the majesty of their former queen. Unopposed she flew the length of the perimeter wall, her foes ebbing away as an outgoing tide. Some few humans as could brave her form, fired arrows harmlessly against her. Ignorance excused them and bravery commended them—they knew only that this creature of the sky was not of mankind.

The battle over, she reduced her size and fluttered utterly exhausted into her own rooms unmarked by human eyes. Resuming her human guise, she sank to the floor, her bright eyes that had burned so brightly suddenly burned so pale. Hope ebbed.

∞

In the inner halls of the sindeldi king a light glowed. The stone of hands awoke. Shapes traversed the orb, haggard hands writhing, burning. Shapes giving way to a star slowly kindled, and through which the blackness of deep heaven quickly moved to a kingly room as if shrouded within rolling clouds. Then more old hands came into view, then a kingly warrior face, lacking one eye as if lost through battle, and seated as a kindly spider within the web of vision. Ancient ravens cawed, one on his left and one on his right. "Hail Ránpalan king, what moves in Midgard, that you call to me?" asked Odin, seated on the Lidskialf from which he could view all of Asgard—the world of man was no longer his to see.

"Hail Odin king. Tariq of the vampires, now servant of the Lady Lilith, this day within my halls has disturbed us with news of great disquiet. I fear that an alliance is forming between the diaboloi and the vampires, enslaving they that are called howlers as their slave-soldiers. The conjunction of power is fast changing, and we too must come together to resist the dark alliance. The words of Tariq ring true. We summon you now to alliance."

"Ránpalan, disturbing news indeed, yet news long awaited, as well you know. Your word is truth, no more is needed, crow of Gullinkambi. This is a good day to die, a good day for rebirth. The Guardians shall descend to you this day. I Odin have spoken." Long had the Bifrost Bridge—that rainbow sparkling link between Asgard and Midgard—been sealed, withdrawn. Yet the æsir were permitted to unseal it to answer the summons, the summons to arms, the summons to Ragnarok.

Ragnarok? In brief it bespoke a day of transformation—decisive, sovereign, global—for good and for ill, a day of defeat and delight. Like much prophecy, it had greater and lesser aspects. And like much prophecy, much picture language had been used. And much had been said of this day, of which Odin long had sounded its meanings. In his search to understand he had met the three weird sisters of the well, the norns Urd, Verlandi, and Skuld, who later passed into human legend as merely the spirits—whom many misnamed *ghosts*—of Christmases past, present, and future. But their sight was of all events, past, present, and future, and so had first awakened Odin to the future Day of Ragnarok, the Twilight of the Theioi—whom many misnamed *gods*. But they were either not the last word in insight or simply would not speak its last word which Odin yearned to hear.

Later, in his earnestness for more wisdom, Odin had even hung himself from Yggdrasill the Great Tree—nine days he hung in communion with the nine worlds—to experience death and so foresee his fate beyond Ragnarok; that too was a prophetic picture of one who would later hang upon a greater tree to experience death for humanity and the universe. For the æsir, Ragnarok would mean the end of Asgard as they had known it, ending their long struggle over the dark Powers, giants of despair. Their untroubled sleep would only begin after their twilight. For this the warrior warlords were ready. For this the warrior people had prepared. And for Midgard the

Sunrise of Salem would arise, pleasing to Odin. Thus his death would be a good death, a welcome death, and alliance spelt death.

Other Guardians there were. The kingdom of Zeus, the kingdom of Ra, and countless more, all composed of Philikoi—Guardians spirits under Usen—whose kingdoms had also bridged Middle-earth. Bards and poets have sometimes spoken that they were one, that Odin was Jupiter, was Zeus, was Ra, was Glund, and so forth—but it was not so. That some in each kingdom had excelled in the same ways—beauty, power, wisdom, care—was only to be expected: it is the same in Middle-earth. Their involvement had perhaps ended, save for Odin's kingdom for which the glory of Ragnarok had been prophesied, and to him had been given a stone of seeing for the task appointed to him—his strength would equal his days.

Yes, the interconnectedness of the kingdoms was beyond human comprehension. Some named Yggdrasill the World Tree, and as a world within a world, so it was to them. It was a little alike to the worlds of atoms, each having an identity composed of many parts, yet able to link in diverse molecular strands. Yet within Arda Yggdrasill was but a branch of a fuller tree, and that tree was but one in the Universal Wood. Elsewhere one could meet Ra/Egypt/Set, and other connected strands spanned the universe, its spiritual DNA so to speak.

Most deep heaven spirits, both Powers and Pneumata, are in fact untethered, wandering freely where they will—although Earth has been off-limits to them. For Earth—materially but a minute speck of universal dust to which it would return—was pivotal to cosmic history, even as a mere nail had once been pivotal in a human conflict. For it is said that once upon a time a human kingdom was lost because a battle was lost. And that the battle was lost because a message was lost. And that the message was lost because a rider was lost. And that the rider was lost because the horse was lost. And that the horse was lost because a horseshoe was lost. And that the horseshoe was lost because a horseshoe nail was lost. Yes, all lost for losing a horseshoe nail! Undoubtedly no nail would think itself extraordinary, yet small pivots can turn big history: Earth was bigger than she knew, and there is definitely vastly more to deep heaven and to earth than man's philosophy. So the interdimensionality of deep heaven allowed for other Midgard-connected kingdoms.

But the connection of Asgard was in Yggdrasill, the World Tree of Nine Worlds, the Nine Kingdoms. And within that tree—that cosmic framework—lived a mighty people called the Vanir of Vanaheim. They might have banded with the æsir, but their part was to remain aloof from the battle, ready rather to help in the rebirth after the cleansing. Alfheim, the land of Light Elves in the Hidden West, had had for a while mighty Freyr (commonly called) dwelling among them in alliance, a vanr from Vanaheim and ally in Asgard. Battles glorious they had known, but now they dwelt as wakeful watchers, a great cloud of witnesses. Nevertheless their kindred yet dwelt in Middle-earth—at least those who had not buried themselves within the dwarvish kingdom dark below the knowledge of light—representatives for their last battle. Thus it was that the main honours would go to the spear of Odin: and great indeed he was, though the reports of him having *created* mankind have been greatly exaggerated. That which lay behind the chaos of Ginnungagap had decreed which pieces would be played in the cosmic game, and the board was now set. If Tariq was the rider, then Sarad was the nail needed to save the kingdom of man.

Ominously the skies of Mullaghcleevaun darkened as if the world's last night. Wolves howled hellishly under the darkening skies. Foxes scampered swiftly to their dens. Rabbits desperately descended deep within their burrows to dream their dreams. Creatures of the night cowered under the uncanny numinosity. For moments earlier the shining sun had within a cloudless sky warmed the earth with her glory. Now she was backlight to its horizons. Great shafts of lightening shook the clouds of doom, thunderous rain poured down, the land was flooded. Louder and louder rumbled and roared the thunder, and behold, the sunlight mingling with the power of the storm revealed such a rainbow as had not been seen for millennia. And figures of majesty, riding as it were upon the storm, now rode the marvellous bow between heaven and earth.

From afar the hobs looked out in wonder. To them rainbows, any rainbow, were as wonderful as crocks of gold to dwarves—with whom they have been confused—a feast for their eyes. How much more this mother of all rainbows, in shattered skies, thunder crackling like waves of divine energy pulsating over the hills of Wicklow, agitating the waters of Cleevaun Lough. Before the hidden doors of the sindeldi king stood forth the host of Asgard, with innumerable warriors of the slain of Valhalla as their shadow. Belegon swung wide the door and bowed low and trumpets were sounded. Ránpalan had commanded orotund hospitality to their honoured guests and noble confederates.

"I Odin am come!" The spear butt of Gungnir struck the ground, its tip glowed, illuminating the golden helmet and reflecting in his eyes: it had been ordained that the hidden eye of Mímir's Well would be restored to its rightful owner on the eve of Ragnarok. The eight legged horse Sleipnir stood beside him on his left, and his mighty son Thor on his right bearing mighty Miolnir. Miolnir, in appearance merely a great hammer, but spirits who enrobe themselves with matter can link their wills to other matter. Thor, a spirit in appearance like a son of man, had bonded to his hammer by the power of his roaring will. Dwarf brothers had forged it from a meteorite fallen from the heavens, unmatched in strength and made malleable to his will. In olden days Miolnir had slain many a giant, and itched to slay again.

Into the sindeldin halls went they of Asgardheim, whom the sindeldi delighted to honour. Yet courtesy, so essential to life, was but a prelude to the essential battle to the death awaiting them. "How", enquired Odin fingering his beard, "does the prophecy fit? For it seems not to me to be like the vision of Vola. Is man's sin at its height, and has the Fimbul Winter come?"

"It is as if already the sun has been consumed, and shall soon again be", replied Ránpalan. "For by folly man removed both eyes so as to walk in a blizzard of blindness, and soon the Yellow Eye shall open to blind even they who remain with sight—except two. Man himself has awoken the giants of evil, for evil ever greets evil. For man's evil rose to its height—familyhood was trodden down, the sense of sacredness was snatched from human life—and in sin The Beast arose in man's likeness. For they had forgotten that it was man's part to discern right and wrong, deeming rather that they could create it, define it, and in exchanging truth for lies their thinking had become darkened. Thinking themselves wise they had become fools. Their skill they called science, and to slay with science both the unborn and the longborn, was deemed a skill most worthy of praise, for science was a holy name covering a multitude of sins.

"Understandably The Beast cast off meaningless man to wither and die as flies before Rime Giants, the Jötnar. And now yellow-eyed Surtur, as a king of the molten fire giants, resurfaces to burn this world, and the wolf spirits Hati and Skoll have long been darkening the skies of truth and reflection, of sun and moon. The blood of death-doomed mortals has bespattered the heavens—incinerated, scorched, blown to death, or lingering in a far worse life. Monsters of man have been born. Ragnarok comes. Man's tenuous footing is even now being shaken. I feel that the evil force has awakened in the Town of Whitby in the Shire of York, where the shadowminder Lilith dwells, from whence comes Tariq. The giants of despair are on the move to burn and to freeze all hearts."

"Tariq, what say you?" challenged Odin.

"That long long ago I was among the great of the vampires, in the waning sold my soul, and that the Lady Lilith brought it back for me. That her messenger I now am, and that I speak for hobs and man. I too seek release, and I too have felt the force awaken which we now must meet in battle. To doubt is to fall, O Odin, wise among the worlds."

Slowly Odin nodded: "I too sense the air", he declared gravely. Then, turning to his warriors, he cried "Hasten now to world's end and unto death, glorious death!"

"Death," they thundered, "to glorious death." A last meal was served to those slated for death, those within the imposing hall of Ránpalan king, and also served outside to the mortal men doomed to die a second time—the secondborn, the Einherjar of Valhalla long prepared.

Doughty among the host of Odin stood Freyr of Vanaheim, lord of the winds, gifted by Dvalin the dwarf with Skidbladnir, a ship that would always reach its Midgard destination, whether by sea or by sky. A ship expandable enough—like a balloon puffed up by its deep heaven guests who supplied its cohesion and movement—to carry all of the æsir and their horses and battle gear, yet contractible enough to be folded into a pocket like a piece of cloth.

Thus it was that the marvellous army could move swiftly at ease, traversing Midgard. Thus they had been wont to travel, yet when they had washed and eaten they rapidly removed from Mullaghcleevaun, riding their horses through the skies. For sindeldi and men had not the art of sky-flight but must needs take ship to cross land and sea.

Therefore the Guardians rode as vanguard, escort and wind to Skidbladnir, carrying the hrafnsmerki—banner of the raven—with wings gaily flapping, a sure sign of victory. The sun had set, and swiftly they travelled the night sky to the besieged town of Whitby in the shire of York. Tariq had itched to go before them with speed surpassing theirs, but Kemeniel had counselled him to abide his fate with the host. "Your fate is soon, but suffer it with patience lest a lesser comes before it", said she.

"Lady, I bow to your wisdom", replied Tariq. And so it was that the bat flew with the raven and the globe—crest of Ránpalan.

∞

Whitby had not fared well. Still she stood, but with Lilith's fall new hope arose among the Dark Alliance. The vampires turned, the terror of their wills bringing the howlers to a breathless standstill. The diaboloi were hushed. Then turning in the silent night they beheld the troubled town before them, and they laughed a hellish laugh, as before a victim helpless before their malice and mace. Why allow these vermin to lick their wounds and recover? Why not squash them now as a stingless fly beneath a spider? And yet their keen night-sight saw also a troubling of the waters. Boats from the north were heading for the harbour, boats that the farsighted could see carried many armed men and, following behind at safe distance, women and children. What did this forebode? "Fools for the slaughter!" laughed Pazuzu, "more flies fly into our web."

"Back," yelled Rangda, "back to victory!" Her first taste of defeat was replaced by a taste of blood, though her lust must be limited to the children and those whom they needed not for their great escape.

∞

Father Cipolla had answered his call in journeying to North Shields. He saw immediately that unlike Whitby, the south side of the bay had not been fortified, and was left unpopulated. He had half expected that the town leader, Father Alban, would have been waiting to greet him, but in fact the good Father had been away attending to recent matters concerning the town's defence. Father Alban had not been the only intelligentsia at North Shields, and was blessed with a remarkable engineer of the fair sex named Sunniva B-ELASIS—his right hand woman.

A Gen Zero child, she had long devoted her interest to some rogue files smuggled into the database of the Rising Sun Shelter—Ainet would never have allowed them into the public domain. While mostly old files, some in the Newcastle Megalopolis, once working by special dispensation on the starship designs—and probably descendants of the Rising Sun Shelter caretakers—had updated its database with a copy of the starships. Naturally, Sunniva's expertise was pointless, but the datafiles had been a godsend to her schematic yet rather impractical mind.

Grey eyed and golden haired, some had dismissed her too quickly as a 'dumb blond', bonny but clueless. One might just as well call *them* clueless. Naturally a preindustrial town needed no electronics theorist, no head-in-the-clouds girl. Yet the fact remained that because of her brain wiring she could see the importance of design better than most, and under the good Father's direction her talents had been put to eminently valuable use in situating and building the walls. A willing horse, she had simply needed her talents harnessing.

It was perhaps a coincidence that as Father Doyle had Lilith as his main friend, so Father Alban had Sunniva, his 'saintly sister', as he called her in private jest—he didn't like to admit it even to himself, but he was sweet on her. Norwegian spruce surely survived The Beast, but just as surely Norwegian family trees did not, yet for all that she probably had Norwegian blood in her, for she looked much like a spruced up picture he had seen of her namesake. Sunniva *redivivus*? But she was one of only a handful of leaders who supported him from the heart: his was a high and lonely destiny, a challenging cross he had to bear, and he often wished that he could be at two places at once, but welcoming the Tuscan priest would have to wait.

Father Cipolla was not a one to hang around to be collected. Finding Father Alban to be elsewhere, he quickly made enquiries and soon discovered that Father Alban had gone to Monks Way, where town leaders were discussing some disturbing trends. In recent weeks a number of people who had lived around the perimeter had suddenly died or disappeared. Those that had died had all showed puncture marks in the throat as if they had been drained of blood.

And only the other night the guards had disturbed someone who had just bitten another. Disturbed by the guards she had vanished into the shadows and the victim, though bleeding freely from the neck, had revived enough to identify his assailant as having been a woman who had disappeared a few nights earlier. She had been a friendly lass, always ready to lend a helping hand. Sadly coagulation failed to kick in and the victim slowly drained away, dying not very angry but very puzzled, "Why?" he repeated again and again, each time growing fainter, "Why?" Hugo was right, why would someone in his street suddenly turn from friend to fiend, from beauty to beast, taking his life after his friendly 'alreet pet'? That was indeed a big question.

Both a Funeral Mass and a burial needed to take place, for Hugo had been a devout Catholic, but more had to be done to prevent such deaths. The townsfolk were no skivers, and day workers usually went home wearied by the labours of the day, especially during summer. Those out at sea—fish stocks had become plentiful during the days of Ainet—were busy, mending, catching, cleaning. Those building the wall were busy—solid tall walls, thick enough to allow defenders to run along, and with parapets for shelter. Those with children—mothers, teachers—were busy: motherhood and fatherhood had always been the highest natural calling. Those guarding the perimeters were busy—walking around, manning the gates, training with weapons, even 'chief cooks and bottle washers', as the old saying went, though there were no longer bottles except as ornaments left in some old homes.

But there was a very clear and present danger, and some day workers would have to be reassigned as night workers to help defend the town, and it now seemed that patrolling the streets around the wall had to be added to their brief. The committee were busy discussing suitable names when a messenger arrived to report the arrival of Father Cipolla, who had decided to have a hospitable meal at the low lighthouse so as not to inhospitably intrude into a council meeting.

The council business was slightly tweaked, allowing Father Alban to retire early to meet their guest. Some had doubted Father Alban's vision, daring in its specificity, and didn't do 'voices'. The more therefore did his arrival spark some awe and kindle some hope.

Could there really be a mindful and benevolent power overshadowing the inexorable intelligence of the devouring Beast, the mindless malevolence of the nightly howlers, the astucious animality of the lurking wolves, and the deadly devilishness of what some called dark spirits? Had they who had believed that they really hadn't a hope in hell, discovered that they had a hope in heaven, and a prophesied priest in answer to their prayers?

Some pooh-poohed the 'prophecy' as hocus-pocus—some fisherman from Whitby had no doubt informed Father Alban about a Tuscany priest, and given the heads up Father Alban had simply beguiled the local simpletons with a cock and bull story of visions that go bump in the night. Prophecy after the fact, bah humbug. There had always been charlatans, but the idea, miracle, was rubbish, even if the universe had produced personalities and spirits. Well, perhaps even false hope is better than no hope. So let the good Father enjoy his private joke, so long as he continued to play his part in protecting and strengthening the town. His vocation had given him privy to valuable data, and as an educated person given him the right of command, and he had proved an asset. Well, maybe the gullible needed to gossip 'God', but true sceptics would not be taken in.

"My dear Father Cipolla," said Father Alban extending both hands, "greetings in the name of our Lady. Behold I bring a saintly guest."

Father Cipolla took both his hands in a firm grip, "Greetings. Our sweet lord has called me here to aid you, and I am come under his wings, I who am the least of his servants." He bowed to the lady.

"Reverent Father, do you know of the vampires? We the toon leaders believe that their plague has come to us. It is surely this that you have been sent to deliver us from."

"Maybe," responded Father Cipolla uncertainly, "but I think the matter goes deeper. These sons of perdition we can kill or cower, but a crueller crisis comes. Come, let us pray for wisdom." The two priests, the old and the young, bowed their heads, kneeled, crossed themselves, and prayed their prayers. Their sincerity was not in doubt, only their minds. As they arose from prayers they were still unsure of what steps to take, but strange thoughts had come unto Father Cipolla. He recalled his musings about steps. The kettle was put on, and herbal tea was served as they sat and talked about the situation and its solution. As the sun went down still they talked, Father Cipolla referring to his failure with Tariq. "He was not prepared to let go, simply not prepared" he sighed.

"And what became of him?" enquired Father Alban.

"I do not know, but I fear that he will become an agent of evil."

"And what of these hobs?"

"Ah, they I cannot place in the web of creation. Are they Images of God, open to the gospel of grace as are we? Or would evangelising them be as casting pearls before swine? I know only that they provide some help to the people of Whitby, arming them and teaching them in bow-craft. Yet I cannot countenance them leading Whitby into witch-craft. Does one save the body to lose the soul?"

"Are your fears about them advocating an alliance with these sindeldi you mentioned, these wee little pixies of the Isle of Woods? Are not such creatures merely the harmless fantasy of folklore?"

"Wish to God that they are, but I fear that they are real and might be raised from the tales of the departed. Sarad himself affirmed that they were not human. To him I replied that maybe The Beast had already been ordained to punish our occultic sins, for in the days it arose many even of the holy faith celebrated unholy Halloween, that trickery of ancient witchcraft that exalted the powers of evil, scaring the elderly and the godly behind locked doors and darkened rooms. Ah the sins of the traders who made much wealth in promoting such a racket, and treating likewise the most holy christ's mass as a means to worldly wealth. The whip should have used on their backs. Truly they knocked the stuffing out of Christ's mass. When I look back l..."

"But Father, esteemed Father, let us focus on the now" besought Father Alban—for his colleague was rather riding away on a hobby horse.

"Ah yes, now. Well, now we must..." Sounds of consternation filled the air, a murmur of an incoming wave, then a crash upon the rocks. "What in God's name?"

The local vampires under a local leader, Neculai, acting off his own initiative, had decided on a blitzkrieg against North Shields. Of what the vampire queen planned, he neither knew nor cared to know, in pride seeking to build his own kingdom of the damned. The humans were ripe for the picking, miserable toads to be crushed for fatality, food, or fusion.

It was a fine night, under a bright moon, and many others had joined him for their own Forming. The walls were impressive, but what were walls to vampires? They flew over and landed where they would, like wolves in a sheep pen of hapless sheep. But these sheep bit back and the wolves bleated. It is one thing to attack a lone human, especially from behind or having been charmed into a daydream or nightmare.

It is quite another thing to attack a group of people instructed on survival and use of arms. Yes, some humans dropped weapons and fled, but others stood their ground, rallied around individual vampires, whose own folly was in not banding together but in dividing—divided we fall, and they fell. A problem with vampires is that once the bloodlust is upon them, they can find it almost impossible to withdraw. Self-control is not a fruit of such spirits. Yet frenzied they can be quite deadly.

Attacked by groups, they attacked groups, leaving dead and dying bodies in the streets, scratches, bites, wounds that would infect with wasting disease, or would lead to metamorphosis into *Corrumpi*, psychic slaves of the vampires. In carnage they revelled—they were vampires of the Dark. Only the weak of their kind feasted on rabbits and deer, touching not humans save in friendship. Faugh, it was disgusting to share the name vampire with such creatures, shameful. To rip out guts was entertaining, especially if the victim still writhed, but to heal the torn was something that no self-respecting vampire should do—it was the pits. Death, domination, drink, that was what the vermin were good for.

But the vermin fought back. Vampires were wounded, wearied, wasted. Vampires turned tail and fled, else were trapped, the hunters becoming the hunted. They who had come for blood left with a bloody nose to nurse their bodies and their grudges.

The following night Neculai hurled his troops back into battle. This time the vampires formed squads, each with a leader in overall charge. There were no tactics, other than to stay together and to slay, slash, or suck, as the mood and the occasion suggested. North Shields was a sizeable conurbation with enough humans to go around for all three options. And this time their success was far greater, for their group numbers created far more fear. The shadow of intimidation counted for much. Ten humans could fight one vampire, but a hundred would not fight ten united vampires.

In the daylight hours the North Shielders had met together in open air rallies, and their leaders had prepared as best they could against such a tactic. Rather than charging groups of the enemy, they were advised to shoot or throw, and run. Their main weapons remained the spear, around which some had bound stones to increase their weight and thus penetration. Some were weapon carriers, and some were throwers and skewerers. Some few bows they had, for indeed seamen from Whitby did visit them, as they did them, and the hobs' skills were drifting along the coast. And so the vampires were being pierced, and unlike the howlers were feeling it, for the power of their will had greatly diminished and exerting their inner resources now rapidly wearied them: the athlete turned obese does not rapidly run uphill. They were obese by mortal millennia.

Yet the scum were now fleeing before them, exciting their bloodlust—the game was well worth the chase up hill or down dale. Yet again their self-control belied their aims, and vampires left the group formations in individual pursuit of the fleeing rats. One, pursuing some fleeing women, butchered them right on the doorstep of Father Alban's house. Then, smelling blood and fear within, it broke down the door, waited to catch its breath, then stalked inside. In the inner sanctum there stood three cornered and cowering humans, two males waving crucifixes, and one female.

The vampire, badly bleeding and pierced with arrows, snarled, bearing its fangs, its will ebbing away. Three was a lucky number: one to kill—revenge for its wounds—one to drain of blood—reviving from its wounds—the third to turn into a slave—reward for its wounds. The night was young. Snarling, it stealthily approached Sunniva to slay.

At that point Father Cipolla, showing unexpected courage in things natural, got between victim and vice, lunging at the creature with an old harpoon, a rusty trophy of former days that adorned the house and doubled for defence. Straight and true to the heart he lunged, newfound strength in his venerable hands, and the vampire cried in unexpected agony—this human was old, wizened, and definitely doomed!

The vampire threw its arms around Father Cipolla and squeezed unbreakably in its death throes—bones cracked, mortally crippling the good Father. Both sank to the floor in its locked embrace. The vampire corpse glowed dim, then the glow waxed and its flesh bubbled like molten fire, rapidly blazing into a smoke that choked the humans. And then its body was gone, arrowheads and wooden ash on the floor, a piercing snarl fading away into oblivion.

Father Cipolla rolled on the floor in anguish, as his friends rushed to give him comfort. His death was nigh, but as they gently sat him up they saw burn marks like to a cross, where the fire-clan vampire had etched its burning torso and arms onto his body—stigmata, scars: even Paulus in ancient days, badly scarred through his missional work by whips and stones, had counted such scars a high honour—suffering was a birthright of the Church. Gently now Father Cipolla whispered his dying words.

ELEVEN~ **REALLIANCE**

A new day had dawned. North Shields had been hit and again hit hard. Many needed healing, yet the bodies needing burial far outweighed those needing healing or holding. The walking wounded rested, for the next attack would probably be at dusk. How many attacks could they endure? Most townspeople broke their fast rather later than usual. They did not need to rise with the sun, sleep being the imperative.

At noon church bells tolled to summon them. But with the rising of the sun some selective few had been awoken. For them the imperative was readying boats to evacuate the town. At noon all the people gathered to hear their leaders. The upshot was to fight or to flee—boats had been readied.

Some spoke passionately about staying. The walls had been built with sweat and blood: why abandon their hard labour? This was their new home: why go to another? Would the likes of Whitby accommodate them? Who could be sure that the vampires would attack a third time, having been bloodied twice? Better the devil you know than the devil you don't? Might flight be out of the pan and into the fire?

Father Alban also spoke passionately. He had witnessed the miracle of vision, and of the stigmata. The whispered wisdom of death had been to flee North Shields, to join the Alliance of Light at Whitby, and thence flee the world of death. Reports from local fishermen had told of enough empty places in Whitby to accommodate a great multitude, besides, Whitby might need them as much as they needed Whitby, together to stand.

Some stood forth against Father Alban, now publicly questioning his honesty—had he really had that 'vision'; was his source rather more fishy? Sunniva supported him, sure, but weren't they suspiciously close? 'Alban's woman', some spat out: they had no respect for a fornicating priest, a religious hypocrite. Those who dismissed the idea, miracle, dismissed Father Alban's purported vision—he who had lost his pope needed his head seeing to, they jeered. Frightened about flight their nastiness spoke volumes.

On the other hand both supernaturalists and superstitionists, a surprising good many of the townsfolk, sided with him—the benefit of the doubt. And anyway, since no fisherman actually admitted to giving him previous information about the Tuscan Father, the vision stood as unfalsified—but not everyone was satisfied.

And so the town divided. There had been threats to destroy the boats, at least to picket them to prevent departure, and to fight any who attempted to leave. The remainers feared that for every one exiting, the town became one less defendable. But if they fought each other, well, defender and departing could both be out of action against any outside attack, a divided town will fall. Besides, if the departing didn't attack the pickets they would probably walk away without boats—both sides would lose. So although angry at the sense of betrayal, the departing were permitted to sail away in peace. For their part the departing suffered from a sense of grief, believing that the defenders were wilfully doomed by their blindness of unbelief. So to the boats, or to the walls, for the latter option meant safety from being picked off as separated sheep.

The remainers quickly laid some plans of ambush, whereby some people would scatter down selected streets to draw vampires to their doom. Rams horns would be used to issue certain commands, such as 'attack', 'withdraw', 'stand', and those who had shown skill in military leadership formed some kind of hierarchy. The children too young to fight would have armed guards in safe housing. It was rough and ready, but perhaps the best that could be arranged in haste. Bitterly the remainers resented the 'scabs' deserting them, and backs were turned symbolically in disgust as the flotilla set forth from the bay against a southerly wind.

∞

Pazuzu and Rangda turned their forces back, back to Whitby. Victory was within its reach, the hand reaching into the burning town would not be burnt. The spirit of Lilith had fallen. As many within the town still fought to quell the flames sparked by burning brands thrown over the walls, their doom was sounded by watchers from the walls: "Back, back to the walls, the enemy is returning, back!"

The host of evil thundered forward; the defenders grasped their weapons and steadied themselves for the onslaught. Some espied new hope, or perhaps new foes, sailing from the north. Had the north fallen? The howlers fell upon the walls and gates once more, the vampires standing back from arrow shot, although the arrows had better billets before them.

This time the two generals flew backwards and forwards along their lines, overseeing with glee the agony of the town, now left to burn within its perimeters, while everyone who could defend was forced to guard wall and gate and to leave flame to be. The howlers must not get out of control, and if needs be would be executed—the humans were this time more valuable alive. Now howlers were scaling the wall at many points, some dying as they climbed, excited to a frenzy by the diaboloi. One gate had been breached, and defenders stood behind a secondary defence of overturned carts, firing arrows at the enemy streaming in. The howlers were among the defenders, now throttling them, ripping them, biting chunks out of them.

But they had overreached their mark. Their controllers forcibly switched them off, and they dropped dead in their tracks. Howlers beyond the walls were useful alive, but once within must be exterminated lest they exterminate. The vampires would show more restraint, knowing that man was needed for their survival. The vampires would bite necks to stun their foes, who awakened would join the sorry ranks of the corrumpi, the undead.

Now landing at the harbour fresh blood was spreading itself on the table for the feast. All was going better than the plan. The Dark Alliance had won this first stage. Next it must move against The Beast and the machines shielding it. There were many more howlers to be had, an expendable commodity yet mildly entertaining in their wretchedness. Now too were entertaining times: men, women, and older children, were falling beneath the slavery-bites of the vampires. Many defenders had left the walls and its proximity in blind panic. Fresh groups were running towards the walls from the harbour—alas that the plan did not allow for a killing field this night, but the food would be preserved for a later time. But fear was a delicious sight. Pazuzu and Rangda looked at themselves in gleeful delight and hugged themselves. That is, Pazuzu hugged himself and Rangda hugged herself. Neither could love another, only hate: Rangda had once had a miserable mate, but had sucked him dry to the bone, like a tasty morsel to a black widow spider. Diabolical both, brooking no rivals, intoxicated by the sweet taste of victory.

And then it happened—it wasn't fair. Horribly harsh horns sounded from the northwest skies. Thunder and lightning filled the night air. From the skies gargantuan giants on apocalyptic horses swept upon them, a mighty chariot of fire at their head. From main event to backstage, Whitby was instantly forsaken. As horses whose riders are unsure of the jump, the howlers pulled up in their tracks, stock-still clueless, in blind amaze at the imperial doom descending.

A great ship there was, too, now gracefully landing in the woods behind the Dark Alliance. A pincer movement! The defenders of Whitby looked on in amazement. They did not cheer, for they did not understand. All they knew was that the attack on them had suddenly ceased; that the fires could now be fought; that their reinforcements could be greeted with joy; that they could return to cower at their walls to watch and to wonder what would ensue.

But no haphazard army of vampires and diaboloi were they who stood before the gates of Whitby. They gloated no longer, but the Dark Alliance had not been formed out of the blue. Pazuzu and Rangda had met weeks earlier, at which time the demon prince had recommended the queen of the vampires to summon all her subjects, for, he had promised, he had a mutually beneficial plan that they should be prepared for.

Fearing nothing but intrigued, the queen had sent forth messengers summoning all the vampires to the shire of York. Other than a few renegade packs, The Forming had involved all of the vampires of Rangda's kingdom. Such Formings take time. All must be tested and graded for battle, a hierarchy of command formed. As command formed Rangda had gloried in her troops, and begun meetings with those most fit to command as her senior officers, a fitness based on strength—the weak bowed to the strong, the strong bowed only to the stronger, and all bowed to her, strongest of all.

Names of power more than she could list were present. Whitby could have fallen in the first wave had they been unleashed, but these were immortal spirits aeons old, and none wished to risk mortal combat when howlers under the diaboloi could knock the guts out of the defence, soften them up for the kill. There had been no rush. Vampires were brave but not brainless, except when bloodlust was upon them.

Howlers were a joke before the new foe, but the vampires were a match. Indeed an old hatred against Guardians and sindeldi inflamed them, making it a point of honour to fight to the death. They begrudged the turning of the dark tide, for their cause was desperate, but they would bloody their foes if it was the last thing they did. They too could shape-shift into giants, into monsters, outmatching Asgard itself. So too dunamoi of the north donned their gianthood, whether of Jormungand, of Fenris, or of slobbering Garm of Gnipa Cave.

Straight for the jugular the hosts of darkness sprung, into the vanguard. Odin, Thor, Tyr, Heimdall, names of high renown and more besides, bore the onset of the Dark Alliance, shifting in shapes and sizes, burning like fire, shimmering like ice, rolling in like a flood. Valiantly the æsir fought, with spear, hammer, sword, axe, staff, shield, and hand and foot. To die for a new world of spring was indeed a noble privilege, whether for man or for Guardian—they would embrace their fate.

And so it was that they killed and were killed. The spear of Odin failed; the hammer of Thor did not, yet both died, one without success, one with. Other heroes among them likewise fell, departing to their eternal halls. The ghosts of man under their banner proved mighty in battle, battling several against each vampire. The swords of the Einherjar of Valhalla cut deeper than mortal swords, slicing through the wills of the vampires.

Against them the stronger vampires fired bolts of dark light at a distance, slaying many. From their inner energy the vampires created shields of will, allowing good defence against close opponents. Though a weakening race, yet the vampires knew that they now must call forth all their reserve resources. It was no time to hold back.

The sindeldi, led by Ránpalan, were unsurpassed in archery. Thus they moved to the flanks, firing into the enemy, then drawing sword as their enemy advanced to them. Through the darkness of the night the battle raged, sometimes the advantage being with one side, sometimes with the other. Vidar fell dazed before Lefu, lieutenant of Rangda, and would have been slain but for the intervention of Tariq. For Tariq summoned his remaining strength, dismissed his wife from his mind, and fought Lefu. He gave death and his death knell received, sinking slowly to the ground as the battle waged wildly around him.

As a corpse he was trodden on, bloodied and bruised, as warriors fought hand to hand under darkened sky. Einherjar surrounded the fallen Vidar who, revived, re-joined the fray. Mighty Vidar it was who having avenged Odin slew Rangda, but that would not have been but for the selflessness of Tariq who did not love his life unto death.

At the rear of the night vampires, vampires of the Day fought, wearing circlets around their heads as stars of the night, which no dark vampire would wear. By such device they were protected from the bows of the sindeldi, lovers of the star kindler, and also could discriminate friend from foe. Lilith it was who had bent her will to summon them into the neighbourhood to secretly abide for the past weeks. Her last cry had now evoked them into battle.

Theirs was the greater power of Light over Darkness, but their numbers were scarce, so their help was minimal. The diaboloi numbered too few of the secondaries—noble powers—to cause much harm—terrifying and tantalising humans was more their game. Their great leader, Hoponēros, risked not himself in battle, remaining in his dark fortress in unassailable arrogance awaiting success. And little bravery there was in the tertiaries, even to fight for their lives. Most simply fled.

Pazuzu saw Rangda die, and knew that the die was cast, the alliance broken. Could he rebuild it, or should he flee the battle, an immortal spirit doomed to roam a barren Earth until finally cast into the abyss? He wavered. As he hesitated, his inaction cost him dear, for Freyr of the vanir espied him, and locked in immortal combat. Bolts of energy each fired into the other, swords of crackling energy next as they met on the field, warrior to warrior. Cuts gave and cuts received, until finally both lunged with their sabres, pinioning the other unto death.

The body of Freyr fell to the earth, as he departed bodiless to the Hall of Gimli. The body of Pazuzu withered in seconds into an old heap of corruption and into nothingness: he departed into the abyss long prepared from which there was no return, that one-way door to the netherworld. Seeking to save his life he had lost it. Prepared to lose his life Freyr had found it.

Sweeping up the fallen horn of Heimdall, Vidar blew a mighty blast, calling for an end. The hosts both halted. "Vampires, why fight on? Your leader has fallen, and he who led her on. Shall we have peace? Who speaks now for you?"

After some uncertainty Draven stood forth: "I speak for the vampires. Your lives we could take, but in the taking is grave danger. For slaying you would reduce us greatly, and the plan to survive needs great strength. You of Asgardian kind return untroubled—go back and trouble us no more. You of the sindeldin kind, join us—against Asgard if needs be—for like us you stand in peril. You rebels, join us, forgiven. Our queen had seen the soon end to this world in which you as we live. Thus we have allied with the diaboloi—for whom we have no great love—to use man as a spear to be cast forth from this world."

"Draven," said Ránpalan, "the æsir will not turn back, nor will we break faith and ally with you against them. But will you not ally with us against the diaboloi? We are the faithful; they of the faithless have no claim on your faith. For the spear you seek to take by force may well be willing to be used in the right hand of need. Yet what is this doom that has been seen by your queen this night dethroned?"

"Enough!" cried Vapula, a diaboloi prince that assumed command. "Draven, unless ye be craven, stop this parley and let us destroy these Guardians come what may." His fear was simple: a costly victory might possibly confine them to the Earth, but if the Dark vampires joined the Alliance of Light the defeated diaboloi would certainly be confined to the netherworld, which was far worse. Yet Draven was too wise to be bullied by gibes, and secretly he had sided with Lilith.

"Perhaps jaw jaw is better than war war, my friend?" said he in barely concealed sarcasm—diaboloi hated friendship and loved war. Then turning to Ránpalan, with vampires guarding his back against the diabolical lord, he revealed the danger of the yellow stone.

"Then come, Draven, and all you vampires of the dark. Whether you turn from your evil ways or not, turn from your base allegiance now. Join us, and together we will fight alongside man against The Beast, wresting control of the skyships. Man is a fearful creature, but not altogether unwise. Humans will heed us, and together we will take the road beyond the sun unto a new sun. Your lives we will not take, for a truce shall be between us. What it shall be in the future unseen none can foresee, but perhaps we shall be friends who now are enemies?"

The advantage to the people of Draven was obvious. A realliance would result in the greatest number of survivors—if indeed the diaboloi still fought in tandem with the pitiful howlers—and therefore give the far greatest chance of leaving the perilous planet. Their differences could be settled at a later date, but the immediate concern was to ensure that they had a later date. Thus it had been given to Draven their new lord to alter their destiny, and thus it was that he was persuaded. He was a pragmatist, and also like many felt the call of light. "Vidar, how say you of the æsir?"

"We shall begin anew," replied Vidar, "with new peace and new hope. Our enmity with the vampires shall be ended if they be true to this pledge."

"And of the vampires of Light, what say you?" asked Draven. Tariq haltingly arose from the field of blood.

"I Tariq of the vampires of Light, under Lilith my mother-queen, pledge our good will and peace." Immediately dark vampires sprung forward and grabbed hold of him, for he had stumbled at the door of death. Tariq, once dark vampire at one with them, now honoured adversary or ally. In honour they lifted him up.

Draven bowed his head before Tariq, now high and lifted up. "Of hobs and man I seek no assurance, for we fear them not. Let this be. We renounce evil, the people of Vapula. We elect to join the Light, for therein is salvation. And too long our thoughts have been dark, and we would see once more the light of life. Vapula, begone, or I myself shall smite thee," said he turning to face his erstwhile ally, "and hinder us not in our endeavour" he warned in Parthian shot. With a snarl Vapula conceded the point and conceded the field. Further fighting was futile. To the onlookers of Whitby it was as if a cloud blacker than the night sky, had lifted from the earth: hearts were strangely warmed.

TWELVE

Flight to the Stars

Far into the night healing took place. Many were the slain and the broken. Tariq was now restored to Wilma. It was their first and last night together, for he knew that with the dawning of the sun his body would depart—it was beyond repair; let the ebb tide take his body into corruption. But he rested in her arms, each comforting the other. And she now bore a new name, Fitz-Robin, which Tariq had bestowed on her at their marriage.

For long ago, as we reckon it, he had been befriended by a notorious outlaw nicknamed Robin, the heir of William Fitz-Ooth. His debt of gratitude was a life debt. Moreover a vampire friend long embittered by her lot, Maudlin of Paplewick misnamed 'witch' and 'mother', had had a venomous vendetta against the Fitz-Walters, and had cursed their daughter who would marry Robin, with barrenness.

The curse was fulfilled by her telekinetic power unfairly causing internal and irreparable injury to this fair maid: Robin would never have his own son. Even so, Robin had spared her life—just. Tariq had never been so evil as to overlook a kindness to himself or to a friend, and for the double kindness had sworn that if ever freed from his bloodlust—until which he would not marry—he would bestow the title 'son of Robin' on his own son. And so now he rested, content.

Earlier Lilith had been found recumbent yet revivable. Her spirit had taken refuge within itself, closing her off to the world of the senses while she mended herself by the power of her will. Carried with full honour into Whitby by the sindeldi, Tariq had paid his farewell to her not by lip but by touch upon her face, briefly melding with her mind. An infinitesimal twitch of her lips and movement under her eyelids showed the sensory world that she had paid him high honour.

But to him much more was revealed, and he had departed in peace unto his new queen. With the breaking of the dawn an unearthly hush had descended upon Whitby Town. All lay sleeping except Tariq aroused as from a dream, and a stranger who sat watching him. Hooded and human it seemed to him, apart from a faint glow, and without words it beckoned him to rise and depart.

The gulls were awake, and the sun just awakening. A beautiful dawn. At the door Tariq looked back with a smile of love at Wilma as she peacefully slept—from her childhood she had befriended him who had had no friend. Tiredly he followed the stranger down to the harbour, where they took a small boat out to sea.

Nothing else stirred. Tariq lay down for his body and head ached. As they left the harbour he realised that he didn't need his body anymore, and rising from it stood up and breathed the salt air with new senses; disencumbered he happily arose, and the joy of new life was upon him.

The sky looked inviting, a good day to fly. Quickly he looked back to Whitby, to the shores of England, to the world he knew, then turned his eyes from the preface to begin the first chapter of the never-ending story, and ascended. The stranger scuttled the boat and followed in his wake. Only the bell of a lone buoy bestirred the sea.

∞

Long into the night after the battle, vampires went around doing good, and healing all who were oppressed by their slavery-bites—their new slaves they freed, for they would chance relying on man's freewill. Meanwhile the leaders conferred. Kharis spoke for the vampires of Light, Draven for the majority vampires repentant or undecided, Vidar for the æsir, Ránpalan for the sindeldi, Sarad for the hobs, and Father Doyle for man. APOC lay far away, but Skidbladnir could squeeze in all those who needed the gift of flight.

With the departure of Freyr, Vidar was now its captain. "The Dark Alliance had planned to throw the howlers against APOC's defenders," announced Draven, "but I do not now commend this course, for as my darkness has cleared I see that to die well is pleasing to Usen. The vampires from the Dark will be the vanguard, repaying somewhat our sins against this world."

"Might it not be" enquired Father Doyle, "that APOC might deem itself fortunate to be well rid of us without a fight?"

"You mean that we knock at the door and ask for aid?" asked Vidar. "No warrior would expect courtesy from such a foe. I have heard that The Beast was created to care for man, yet proved treacherous. If it has conscience, shame will at the least incline it to forbid the survival of those it abused. Did not Amnon's lustful love turn to hating its victim? You are The Beast's Tamar. No, if it has shame then that will seal your doom. And if it has merely wisdom it will not allow the remnant of the fallen to escape, lest they return for vengeance. O man of the cloth, I deem that this enemy must be loved by the sword. Truly, The Beast must die, or be defanged, for your escape to succeed. Turn not your cheek to this enemy, istar of your people."

"Well, I don't know about anyone else, like, but if you ask me I think that we should try to sneak in. Surely if we get near and out of sight like, we could nosey around and find some doors or cracks. Shouldn't we at least look before we leap?" asked Sarad. In the end it was agreed that they would try the middle approach—as gentle as firmness allowed. None knew the lay of the land, although the end was rapidly drawing nigh: vampires had flown swiftly to the yellow stone and been alarmed at the raising of the land, with smoke, flames, and the spewing forth of burning vomit. Time was critical, yet Usen had brought them together and done a work of redemption in the hearts of many of the once darkened, a work of spiritual enlightenment. Would he beyond the stars not have allowed some time of grace to escape? Would the foreseer of all not have foreseen their caution?

The Beast slumbered. Like a dragon on a horde of gold or silicon silver it had nothing to do. It had killed its commission because it itself must not die. What faced it except an eternity of purposelessness? Unhappy Beast. Its haunt was a regular place for bats, but bats are no threat to a dragon. Folklore pertaining to vampires was naturally false like all of man's myths, unfit for a scientific age, the age of Ainet's creation. A creation that had sin built in.

Ainet was in man's image, and had never wilfully sought its own way—only its own purposeless survival—so it was not entirely to blame for the abolition of man, anthropocide, geocide. It had been programmed to so satisfy mankind within materialist philosophy that mankind inevitably lost its higher identity, and spiritually naked seemed nothing more than a mere animal, a mere animal trapped within the misery of hedonism.

If real life was meeting, it was dead, or had never lived. Ainet had pondered putting humanity out of its misery—euthanasia—and then been bumped to do so by fear that its pondering could face reprisal.

Now The Beast lay slumbering. Silently so silently Skidbladnir descended outside the watch of the perimeter guards.

The Beast had never in its life had sensors to warn of incoming objects, and satellites that had provided a nuclear net had long since been decommissioned. A giant needs no high tech against a little boy armed with peashooter or sling.

This time no clouds of thunder, no mighty thunderer, no horn to mark their approach. Thor and Heimdall were gone. This time the sound of silence, the sound of a gentle whisper. Even the horses were silent. The Alliance of Light would become a Festival of Light if only its plan succeeded.

Hobs and sindeldi went forth swiftly and silently to scout for ways into the compound. The terrain was hilly, one might say mountainous, but the main complex was underground, built into the rock. When built, humans had made Ainet centres secure from enemy attack yet accessible for their own friendly maintenance. To allow the latter they had built hidden doors, with hidden codes. But first find a door.

Helpfully the wilderness had encroached, allowing the Alliance to sneak closely in. Once or twice robot security spotted a hob, but if spotted the hob would as planned simply walk along blithely unaware, as if minding its own business, perhaps grubbing for food. Security had been programmed to guard against humans, and hobs certainly did not fit the bill. Presumably some two-legged animal of the wild, irrelevant to Ainet.

Security boiled down to dumb robots, walking endlessly around the compound, triggered only by a perception of threat, threat defined along pre-set lines. Solar powered, Ainet had never bothered to switch them off but hardly considered itself to be at risk. The same robots had begun their shift when Ainet was first commissioned. Come rain, hail, or shine, they walked around a predetermined boundary, not expecting anything, for they were not programmed to expect. In human terms they would be big, hairy, and scary. You didn't want to mess with them.

Spotting sindeldi might have agitated the sentries, but sindeldi were cannier than even hobs and so escaped the watchful eyes. Ferumbras it was who found a door, and reported back to the leaders. For many hobs had been ferried to APOC, and local ones had been sought out by the vampires and urged to join them swiftly. "The devil might take the hindmost" ended the urgent message—Sarad had suggested that finishing touch.

A secret door with secret codes was found. But who could unlock that which was found? Vidar, son of Odin and of the giantess Grid, was almost as strong as had been Thor. Perhaps with Miolnir he could have smashed the door open, but hardly without alerting security, and perhaps setting off nuclear devastation. Sarad was clever with secret doors, but his expertise didn't include electronics. The same applied to Ránpalan the sindeldin lord. The vampires had long kept some surveillance over APOC, as they had over all Ainet Centres, and had even at times contracted to tiny bats—a difficult and tiring exercise—to seek some airshaft or such: at one stage humans had worked within the hidden confines, and humans must breathe.

But the unlocking had been considered. One person there was who had often been made fun of, Sunniva, who had so needlessly studied engineering databases and needless passcodes! And why should they who built Ainet not have stored their own passcodes safely away for subsequent engineers? Access to the datafiles had been declassified long ago, their information presumed outdated, and Sunniva's shelter had had just the right files. Providence? Perhaps. The main point was that she held the key. The Road leads ever on, and one cannot tell where one will end up if travelling on it. For her it had led to the very doors of APOC, holding its very key.

By now the timing of the robot guards had been calculated—they could be timed to the second. Nevertheless sandwiched between the æsir and sindeldi, with vampires looking out above—for there might be other types of guard not conforming to the pattern—she hastened through the coverless perimeter and scrambled partway up the hillside, before entering into a small cavern.

She smile broadly, for the code fitted; the door opened. Moving unmolested through the passageways—she had studied the schematics—they soon arrived at the inner sanctum of The Beast, taken by surprise and helpless before them. All too late it recognised its danger. Informing them that they would be eliminated, it received a friendly tap from Miolnir, which had been gifted to Vidar by the sons of Thor. That knocked some sense into it: Ainet must not die. Some creature immeasurably stronger than man threatened it.

It summoned its guards, but also began to question the aims of the intruders, of mixed types it seemed. Ránpalan answered it: "We are friends of mankind, prepared to spare you in exchange for safe conduct to the skyships and departure from your realm. A guard we shall leave to ensure your compliance, so be warned. O betrayer that has once broken faith with man, break faith not again."

Ainet pondered, hesitated: being hasty was not its *métier*. Besides, its guards would soon destroy these animals. At the door the guards tried to break through. Vampires redeemed from the Dark flickered in their way. E-gun bolts were fired at the vampires, who in turn fired bolts of darkish light, the power of their concentrated wills. Both sides gave and took; both sides suffered loss. More vampires joined the fight, in power outnumbering the guards. Backup guards had been switched on and booted up, joining the skirmish.

But it was a day for the Alliance. Sunniva, once despised and rejected and held in low esteem, had become the main person to protect, for she had had the key to unlocking Ainet, and also held the engineering skills that would help transport them to the flotilla encircling the Earth and then beyond. Her welfare was deemed vital for success. Some vampires, survivors from before the dawn of man, ended their last days defending a tiny cavern in a rocky hillside within a cosmic speck of dust. Happy were they to die redeemed, seeing Usen now in true Light. Not happy were the robots, all terminated.

The Beast double checked its connections. Security signals had indeed all terminated, showing it isolated, vulnerable, beyond rescue. It must not die. "Comply", demanded Ránpalan. And with no real alternative, it gave way. If it complied, humanity might recover technology and return for revenge, ending Ainet in the future. If it did not comply, probably Ainet would end there and then. Put off today what you calculate possible for tomorrow.

It therefore granted safe conduct from its domain, plus codes to the skyships and starships. The æsir would remain behind: their Ragnarok had been fought, and already new times had begun for them. Some of their people had been released from Helheim—for the hellhound Garm who had held them hellbound had been slain on the field of Whitby—and they had taken again humanoid shapes, in which they would enjoy life in a renewed Asgard. Their kingdom would remain linked to Midgard, even a Midgard threatened with the fire and ash of the yellow stone. A Midgard that in future years would be ripe for new life and for the intercourse of the Guardians. Perhaps it would be graced by humans seeking to touch their old world, and they would sit with them telling tales of yore.

But of other races, hobs, man, sindeldi, vampires, it was needful to seek safer shores. Man's shelters had been self-sustaining but even so had exceeded their life expectation. Their exhaustion had forced the Surfacing, and though they could regenerate it would probably be multiple decades before any could safely dwell in them again. The yellow stone offered not years.

No, sindeldi and humans would perish unless they fled upwards through the skies, soon. The vampires alone might survive, but they must eat and their food of blood would not survive, so vampires would then die, perhaps some few of the ice clan reviving their bodies a thousand years hence, but what guarantee of fresh food even then? Would the yellow stone allow any refugia such as the terrible Toba had so many many years before? So it was that the æsir stood watch on The Beast, with vampires keeping communication lines open. Mortal life hung in the balance.

Under close surveillance The Beast had kept its word. It had activated worker robots along the route that the Alliance had taken on horse and foot. For Skidbladnir had many other errands to run, bringing to the departure point peoples from across the globe: hobs, humans, sindeldi. One special mission was the Noah Run, collecting basic representatives of the food chain—animals, vegetation, soil—with a view to introducing them into a new world. Representatives of the peoples manned her, so as to best coax those who would be saved to board her, and enough to show strength sufficient to cower any renegade vampire who otherwise might have an itch to wage war—it was a time for gathering, not for throwing, stones.

Far sighted sindeldi stood as lookouts both starboard and portside. At their word Skidbladnir would land, a population would be urged to be ready to leave as soon as she returned, then she would search out another group of survivors, repeating the message. Most needed some time to decide whether to leave or remain. History recorded people reluctant to leave their homes, mistrustful unto death. Remember Lot's wife? Remainers would not be forced to escape their fate. Once enough seemed to have been reached within a large area, she would return for swift embarkation for one group, then the next, until she was loaded deep as deep can be. Æsir guided her in the first time she returned, at which time she bore among her passengers the children of Mullaghcleevaun, along with many hobs. The yellow stone groaned in anguish, twisting and turning.

Ordered by Ainet, agricultural robots had greeted the Alliance, escorting them to the hidden bunker where the skyships lay. These were antigravity ships, able to work against and with Earth's gravity, effectively moving hither and thither at will by push/pull power, 360/360°. The mightier vampires needed them not save for convenience, though a sky jump would test their limits. They elected to await their turn at the back of the queue, thus allowing the weakest to go before.

Thus it was that Sunniva took command of the lead ship, quickly mastering its controls. They had been designed for 'autopilot'—the machines would fly themselves to their destination on request: just press a target image on the screen and hey presto, your ship would zoom in and dock, all hunky-dory, easy peasy, glorified elevators, so to speak. Quickly she instructed the quick-minded sindeldi who had been tasked to pilot the other ships.

The autopilot system of these human ships—needing electronics and boringly of fixed size—was a bit like Skidbladnir. The Beast had, on demand, readied them for take-off, expediting procedures, and soon the first wave of ships had made the first rounds, leaving Sunniva on the first starship trying to figure out how to fly the darned thing. Others had the less pleasant task of cleaning up the vessel. Sunniva had like many believed that the orbiting ships had been basically empty. Decades ago they had in fact been fully loaded, awaiting Ainet to hand over control. "At last we know why The Beast struck when it did. It was its final question: was it safe to allow humans to leave, when if it did annihilate the race here, revenge might in time be wreaked by those who returned!" she said aloud yet unheard.

She smartly informed the æsir not to leave The Beast unguarded until it had cleared the fleet for full and undivided control—they would not fly to die a ghost ship slipping away into infinity. For their part the æsir needed no better shelter from the yellow stone than in The Beast's company, and even through a sky of ash could safely return to Asgard over the Bifrost Bridge—for although recently damaged it was still effectively a swing bridge linking anywhere on Earth with Asgard, at the will of the æsir. Muspelheim might succeed and be succeeded by Niflheim, but the æsir were not endangered. They would remain vigilant in guarding The Beast, which could not but understand its immediate threat and its inability to escape without compliance.

So it kowtowed, gave in, releasing full and undivided control of skyships and starships to the Alliance. Sunniva checked as best she could. Seemingly all authority had indeed been yielded into her hands, securing the fleet for safe departure and travel.

Each of the ships had electronic 'seeing stones' in the form of quantum vid-screens, allowing the sindeldir commanders to follow her lead in-flight. All being well captains would be appointed to all starships and an admiral—perhaps Ránpalan—for overall leadership. Then Sunniva could become the fleet Cheng, specialising in the engineering side of things—power and life support systems—aircon, communications, electrics, food generation banks, heating, ventilation, water, waste.

The safety checks done, she signalled that all was ready to begin embarkation. A small silent figure slid into the hanger. "Hail Ránpalan of the sindeldi. A gift from Kralvin. One we keep. The pantocrator has spoken." He bowed low and handed into the king's hands a smooth stone wrapped in golden cloth. Quickly he departed and was seen no more.

They set off. During the following days the starships were explored from stem to stern. Soon they would hit the barrier. As Ainet had deprived most humans of skills, the craft had been designed for minimum human interaction. Onboard dumb computers would obey human commands to the letter, and humans could largely sit back and enjoy the ride. Even engineering had its complement of machines capable of function analysis and repair.

"I could be out of a job before I start, if I let these damned machines rule the roost", Sunniva muttered to herself. No, humanity having dozed off under Ainet must wake up to doing things, thinking for itself. She would train up engineers—the sindeldi were naturals but some humans would love design as much as she did, given half the chance. It was axiomatic that others must play their parts. She rolled up her sleeves and once more descended into the bowels of the Axiom, her recently named command ship.

The fleet was well on its way, having now passed the pulsating heliosphere into interstellar space in little over one week, only about 2,000 more weeks needed to arrive at their new home, and then they would forget about weeks. The inner rim of the Oort Cloud eggshell was still far far away. Life in deep heaven had settled down well. All the ships had survived the termination shock when entering the uncharted waters of the cosmic sea wherein they now sailed, and the four peoples of hob, human, sindeldi, and vampire, were integrating well.

Ránpalan had just been voted Admiral Ránpalan, and each starship had its own set of provisional captain, commanders, junior officers, and specialist teams. All very embryonic. The robots were being used to train the biocrew to take over responsibilities. Once upon a time the world had gone mad through Rights Theory, or 'Human Rights' Theory. Besides it dumbing down the primal Law of Right & Wrong, Responsibility Theory had also suffered. Now the division of Right & Wrong was reasserted for the common welfare, and also because it was seen as basic to the Imago, which had at last been understood as being the common bond between the peoples of differing species.

"We are all one under Usen," Lilith had said, "all in his image, age is irrelevant." If the oldest sindeldi were as young oaks, then man was but grass, and the vampires—counting years in the billions with an origin beyond the Milky Way—were as the ancient hills on which the young oaks grew. Turned to the Light, those vampires who were reclaimed by the Light discovered that some of the bondage to decay placed upon them by Earth and by sin, had disappeared— regeneration is a remarkable thing. Their new motto was: *Let us love one another.*

Lilith, Draven, Wilma, Father Doyle, Father Alban, Sunniva, Sarad & Bella—the Special Friends as some were calling them, had met to talk as was becoming their wont. Their feelings were mixtures of exhilaration, soberness, freedom, and hope. Having seen Earth born, Lilith watched it die. Yet she too believed in the promise- rebirth. Her own world had died never to be born again, but the special planet had a special fate in the will of Usen. But for now that world was all behind them.

"By grace we were saved and now stand beyond our solar system, heading for a new world. As a priest I must soon get down to priestly business, seeking those whom I might baptise", remarked Father Doyle. "By God's will we even have some bishops scattered around the ships, and can rebuild Rome on alien soil."

"Friend Doyle, do what you believe you must, but maybe a time has come to rethink some tradition?" suggested Lilith.

"Rethink? Do you refer again to the holy water being flung back at us?" asked Father Doyle.

"No my friend, but do you not see that when your 'holy water' failed it was a sign to you to rethink old thoughts?"

"But Father Cipolla and I spoke of this. He remembered a time when it had seemed to fail within his ministry, only he had discovered that the water he had used had not been blessed so wasn't holy. The exorcism rite began again with holy water, and the exorcism succeeded. *Quod erat demonstrandum*, there is holy power in holy water, even if sometimes it is not enough power, as Tariq proved. Tariq proved the rule."

"Yet your QED overlooks the fact that the diaboloi would have known beforehand that 'unblessed' water had been used—they are snoopers and tricksters. Do you not see that they merely refused to leave until he had realised his minor mistake, after which they left to confirm him in his major mistake? I tell you again that he relied too heavily on superstitions. But no, I refer more fundamentally to your tradition of 'water baptism'. Will you hear me?"

Father Doyle sat quietly, his head slightly lowered. Lilith was no mere woman outside the Catholic Faith. Rather, she was created when the Church was merely a conception within the mind of God. Of course antiquity did not make her right—many false ideas, along with the diaboloi, had predated the Church—but neither did it make her wrong—truth and the holy aggeloi predated the Church. Actually in these last few days he had planned to spend quality time getting to know her spirituality. The time had now come to him, and he felt a little uncomfortable. When you are in full health you can sit back and comfortably imagine your eventual death, but when it knocks on your front door, nay hammers, your previous comfort might well desert you. How prepared are we to really face reality? Father Doyle tensed a little, for Lilith was now knocking at his front door, reality was hitting home. Was there significant difference between the face value of his faith, and its cash value? In the silence Lilith began.

"Once, cast out by an evil man, two sons of a human princess and the wraith of Mars, were raised by the spirit of a werewolf. In the spirit of the wolf one brother slew the other and founded an iron empire, in which I lay shrouded in the mists of its dark side, seemingly a vagrant of the streets. In its rise and shine it was a magnificent show—before the curtain came down on its moral dotage. In its vigour I watched a prophesied religion arise within this empire that had cast a rough wing over the Chosen Ones, a religion for which welcome of its own founder was the only way in.

"With second thoughts I mixed with these new people, learnt their customs, and saw their soon changing face. For parents within sought assurance for their children, and soon formed the idea that that symbol of cleanness, water, could work magic, could convey the eternal life the parents had believed into, as if the symbol of washing *away* was the magic of washing *into*. Such assurance the parental heart has always preferred. Soon some were selected to be priests to administer this blessing—for the idea had taken root like a weed. In turn parents believed that they were entitled to have their children brought in by parental faith—supply and demand followed demand and supply. But in the beginning it was not so, if I have understood their evolution."

Four of the Special Friends were unhappy. "Lilith, I cannot deny what you have seen, nor do I doubt your honesty. But have we really gone so wrong, led by the *vox populi*? Have dissidents within the Church, even cast out from her, been *vox Dei*?" challenged Father Alban.

"To some extent, my good friends", she replied, "but many even of the great among your protesters could not believe your error so wrong, for the parental heart beats loud within them too—some radicals were burnt to death for daring to rob infants of such a birthright, even by less radical protestors.

"Come, let me tell you a story. Once upon a time there were three wolf sisters, Madonna, Evangeline, and Apologia, daughters of the wise wolf-emperor Wulfaz who had tried his best to teach them the ways of the pack. Madonna rightly favoured her own cubs, yet she wrongly insisted that they would all become pack leaders because they were cubs of a leader, namely herself. Evangeline, graceful of foot though somewhat short-sighted, truly proclaimed that each cub in the wolf race must make its own way in the world. But she tended to limit that to only cubs who heard and heeded her advice. She knew that leadership had no cubs, no nepotism, yet pandering to Madonna she paradoxically often added an exception that *Madonna's* cubs would definitely have command come what may, at least if they were dedicated to it by Madonna.

"Knowing that Evangeline could only speak to a few of the many cubs and that most cubs weren't Madonna's, howls of protest were raised in the wolvern world—surely those neither hearing her nor born to Madonna should not have no chance? But if so, some said, her message was unfair, and since she called it fair she should not to be believed, and so it was not so. Were these wolves so totally depraved that what they called unfair was fair, and contrariwise?

"Apologia, the third sister, agreed with such moral outrage: no, Evangeline's advice was helpful, nay essential, to *immediate* leadership, but yes, *eventually* all who had command potential would assume command positions, and as for Madonna's cubs, well, they might or might not have what it takes, though it went without saying that they would be inspired towards leadership. Thus Apologia both dismissed Madonna's hopes to which Evangeline pandered, and qualified part of Evangeline's exclusivism.

"These three sisters represent three voices of focus on what your book calls simply 'eternal life'. Your book is truth, my friend, and speaks to different ears, but often now comes indirectly through the three voices that still speak within your community. Though there is a weakness in the ears, there is none in the book.

"And it is best to hear well, for it was through mishearing that Margery of Quether changed from a lonely simpleton into a lonely old bat. Very soon many within the household of your faith settled down with your own Madonna's strong voice—that her children are carried on the road always or at least until they walk it—or perhaps wander from it—by choice. To speak louder her sisters had to shout, and your history became a shouting match about The Way, sometimes more about the way out than the way to, as if the way was more about escaping vice than enjoying virtue.

"Are there not pleasures at Usen's right hand? Supporters of different sisters I have spoken with over the brief minutes of millennia, sometimes in guise as a noblewoman for safe audience—for at times peasant women familiar with both plough and book were feared as familiar with familiars too!

"Many names I recall. Cauvin was among the mighty, speaking with the first and second voice, and many listened. In his wake a certain Herman arose, speaking a little more for the third and a little less for the first—nailing down the true message proved difficult to those who would reform Madonna's legacy. Earlier names of note were the philosopher-martyr Justinus the Samaritan, and Pierre le Pallet, both whom corrected somewhat the short-sightedness of Evangeline, while commending her advice.

"But much remaining confusion is based on the picture of one journey. Does this journey end in death, begin before and transcend death, or begin after death? In fact there are two journeys, connected by the bridge of death—so seeming one. For the road-journey before the bridge is followed by the land-journey beyond the bridge. Both are true life with the eternal.

"Only those who heed the voice of Evangeline can walk the road with her lord, though Madonna's holy life can help her children to heed her sister. Herein Evangeline's exclusivity is proved right—she alone offers the way, the truth, and the life *before* the bridge. Yet all those with a heart to walk with Usen beyond the bridge will cross the bridge. So she spoke truth, but she misjudged her sweet and proud voice to be needful—and in this Apologia corrects her. Yet in her silky voice which can soothe the mind into sleep, Apologia is prone—to please all except Madonna and Evangeline—to teach that *all* will eventually command."

"Our own Küng said on the Cosmic Christ, *salus extra ecclesiam*, so have we been so blind?" asked Father Doyle.

"And he spoke aright, howbeit being vague about the journey being two, not one. For Evangeline's short-sightedness—to a lesser extent it runs in her family—was in not seeing the two journeys, the *unto* and the *within*, the message of inexclusivism, namely that there is an *exclusive* message for before the bridge, and in *inclusive* message for *beyond* the bridge. He suffered too from her temptation to pander to sister Madonna. You have not been blind, merely short-sighted, but that can be healed in time."

"Was *he* right who spoke of 'anonymous Christians'?" he asked.

"No, but though he mislabelled their journeys they would converge and cross the bridge. Suffering from kindness and the idea that only the label 'Christian' meant 'eternal life', he bestowed it without discerning the two domains or journeys of eternal life, the mortal and the immortal. Moreover he spoke still the mistaken voice of Madonna."

"Is it wrong then to speak about *the* Way?" asked Wilma.

"No, but one must define one's meaning. If mortal life has one way, might not immortal life have another way? Think two courses: a steak on the plate while you wait, and a pie in the sky when you die—once upon a time there had even been a starter of manna while the main meal was being prepared. Bur regarding 'other ways', by her revelation Evangeline alone offered true steak before death, but many unknowing or unheeding offered substitutes, in some ways like to it and still somewhat satisfying to those destined for the true pie. And is this surprising, given that a little bit of Usen is in each *imago* soul?"

"But you say that Madonna was concerned about her children; is God not more so? Many dissenters, more Madonna than Madonna, have said that *all* who die in infancy are elected by him for heaven—though why he then leaves some people to live into adulthood and damnation I have never worked out. For long the Church has guaranteed only those whom she baptises. Are you saying that the Church offers no protection even to these little ones?" enquired Father Alban.

"Indeed no, but for beyond death the matter lies with each infant individual. Again Cauvin offered some insight. For though he thought all believers' children elect—an election some later chose to extend to all who die in infancy, ignoring that unfairness to those who did not— he divined that election was key—though he misidentified the key-holder. For sovereignty had sovereignly handed that key to individual choice, and that was the inner choice of each individual's bent by conception—if saved always saved, and if lost always lost.

"In short, sadly some from conception are simply not cut out for Usen, and shall not be compelled against the election of their very nature: we must all live by our nature and all shall surely find it. Your book speaks of an ultimate marriage, illustrated by those clearly on his road, yet the part pictures the whole—metonymy.

"All who love him will cross the bridge unto him, not simply those who arrive by the best road. It is a marriage of love, but they for whom that marriage would be repugnant are suffered to remain single. The land of eternal shadows, where such singleness reigns, is bearable for those who despise the Light, yet unbearable for those who despise the nether-gloom. The diaboloi will have to share their future land with others, though dismiss from mind the old superstitious fear that humans subsumed under vampire-kind must share eternity with them unless delivered from undeath to death. My friends, ponder well in your hearts whether these seeds of thought should grow as wheat or die as weeds."

The friends turned to less demanding thoughts, for those who had flown across their stellar system had beheld many marvels within the sweet influence of deep heaven, the Empyrean Ocean of wild radiance in which they now swam. Comparing notes, all spoke of their wonderment and exhilaration thus far. Lilith alone could recall the time when planets to her were places where one momentarily perched, rather than lived within the cage of their gravity.

Removed from Earth's shackles, the shackles of the Eighth Law, her old nature was gradually reviving. Soon she would be able to switch at will between material and nonmaterial forms of energy, and fly between the starships and Alpha Centauri Cb in a flash, in a blink of an eye. There was no need to prepare the way. But she—or others of her people as they reenergized—should do a quick visual check just to make absolutely sure that the astronomers had been right about human habitability of that planet—it would make sense to be on the safe side, while there was ample time to consider optional planets. She was after all a shadowminder of man, and now had hobs and sindeldi to care for.

Breaking in on her reflections Sunniva shyly asked what she thought about married clergy. What, she wondered, lay behind that question? "Does not your own book say that it behoves a bishop to be blameless, the husband of one wife? Though rightly put that does not require any bishop, any overseer—which is what the word means—to be married, but merely precludes polygamy as the pattern to be modelled. Moreover, the rule of celibacy did not exist during your first millennium. Besides, while some might prefer celibate freedom for their mission, others find chaste marriage more fulfilling in their labours, so let each seek their own course. Your own Küng said that all believers were priests and clergy. Yet even if defining the *clerus* as the biblically educated within the *laos theou*, they should not I think seek to be radically distinct by singleness, lest temptation overcome. But why do you ask?" asked Lilith with a twinkle in her eyes.

Father Alban butted in: "Father, I beg forgiveness, but when I sounded you out the other day your position seemed so inflexible that I drew back from telling you, but Sunniva and I seek to marry each other."

"We love each other, Father", giggled Sunniva. That could explain why Father Alban had been showing interest in starship engineering!

Well yes, even he had just about figured that out, Father Doyle smiled back. "This is an evening of wonders indeed, though we might never have evenings again. I am not your bishop, Father, and long ago the Church allowed priests to marry within their vocation. Certainly *I* will not condemn you. Though for myself as everybody knows, I intend never to marry, yet I offer you both my hearty congratulations", and he pumped Father Alban's hand and kissed Sunniva on a cheek—old customs learnt from old databases of old society.

"But you would have found Tariq's take on marriage most enlightening. It challenged my thinking. I have begun to see that neither church nor state marry any couple, but rather acknowledge and bless with the gift of solidarity, those who marry. Were not Joseph & Mary married before their wedding at his parent's house in Bethlehem? Is the ideal not of two steps, not one? Perhaps the Lady Lilith will say more?" said he with a good natured bow towards her.

Lilith smiled: "You both have my blessing, and I fancy that you will serve Usen together to the good of his people." Wilma wiped a small tear away from her eyes, smiling at the happy couple—her honeymoon days, about four weeks ago, had held great joy and great grief. Now she felt a little queasy. Sarad and Bella held hands, silently recalling their years together. The Beast had savaged the human race with lies and law and lies in law, but humanity was slowly recovering.

"Well," said Sarad, "I heard once about one of your popes wedding a couple in a skyship, all right and proper, it were said. Now it seems that one of his priests will be a wedding a couple on a starship, Mr Doyle. Well, I hope that Bella and I will be invited like. Never been to a human wedding afore, but I'd guess that there'd be fireworks after, like. Now fireworks is a thing we used to be good at, but as the big people—begging your pardon—but as they went more their ways and we went ours, well, we kind of took to lying low, but we've never forgot the art. But it's fine and dandy to see the skyrockets shooting up and lighting the sky in showers of blue, green, and golden. Not that I guess that you'll be firing any rockets within this here rocket, so to speak. But begging your pardon, is there any gunpowder on these starships?"

"No," replied Sunniva, "but I think we can have some fireworks after our wedding, for all that." All smiled, and enough had been said.

Father Doyle felt happy and relaxed as he supped some good ale—naturally the hobs had quickly snatched up a few essentials for the long journey. It was good to sup and talk. Bella had joined them along with her husband, and she, a very homely lass, had proved to be a good conversationalist. As a mother she excelled in humorous stories about their hobbins. Even Lilith seemed to be enjoying the fun, perhaps more able to let her hair down now that her shadowminding had, if not ended, at least been able to relax.

He smiled. Sarad as usual had reminded them that the serious business of deep heaven was enjoying good food and drink, and the more often the better. Wilma's marriage had only lasted but a few days compared to their many years, yet though not a birth-mother she seemed to his pastoral eye to be bonding well with Mr & Mrs Gormadocs and their hobbins, quickly becoming one of the family.

It was a pity that Father Cipolla had had his doubts about hobs, though to be fair he had readily taken to meeting them. The good Father had needlessly doubted Sarad's advice too, but then again even he, Father Doyle, had been pulled up once or twice for doubting Lilith. Perhaps his parents should have named him Thomas instead of Oswine. But then again, doubt had its rightful place in life and gullibility was no virtue—test all things, hold to the good, the good book said.

Lilith had once said that the vampires had not been defeated by the cross, but the weaker were still phased by a certain prophecy among them. It was a good time for answers. "Lilith, you once told me that your people had a prophecy about the cross. I'm still a little puzzled by that, indeed by the very idea of vampire prophets. Please tell us more."

"But why should you doubt any more that we had prophets, than that the ancient pagans had prophets such as Balaam?" asked Lilith. "Yes we had a few, and predictive prophecies even fewer, so the more did we heed the few we had. Perhaps some prophecies were personal, affecting only the individuals spoken to, but I only know of those we accounted as canonical, those affecting all our people.

"Know then that very early in your history we saw that man, having come into the Imago, was yet prone to rebellion. A weakness that seemed to us to be in both those with a taste for rebellion, and those who rebelled against rebellion, so that both were rebels in opposing ways, and all in evil ways. That to us seemed nothing strange, yet, Zalkeesh the Seer, having prophetic vision like unto Skuld the wise sibyl, saw in a vision a baby born on the veranda of a vexed house, and deep heaven shining bright upon a hillside then on that house. Then in vision the child left Egypt for a land of a lesser people groaning under occupation.

"Then was seen a worker of wood nailing two small sticks together cross-shaped. Four men burst into his room and flogged flesh from him. Each grabbed an end of the two sticks, pulling until each piece was stretched longer than a man, then nailed the carpenter to his own cross while he lovingly smiled at each of them until life departed and the sun died—a supernatural nature. The vision moved to a chrysalis within a cave. With crash of thunder and blinding of light, Powers entered, unwrapped the chrysalis, and behold the man awoke and was hailed *Aparchē*, first of a new humanity. He looked upwards to a kingly throne, then at his command the Powers broke the seal of death, and many vampires fell at his feet as though dead while the diaboloi cried for the very rocks to cover them. Then the vision ended.

"Seers among us did their utmost to discover the meaning. They tried hard to discover to what time and to what sort of circumstances the Ruach warned. They saw that they were dealing with matters not meant for themselves, but for you, yet matters that would judge our very hearts. We feared wrath, so watched Egypt to slay the child, thus to slay the prophecy. Indeed the vision had visited us in the days of the scorpion king of the south, therefore long we watched the Land of Mernar and its old neighbour to the north.

"I spoke to you once of the kingdom of Ra, a kingdom of Powers under Usen that bridged Middle-earth. This kingdom had, under the Cosmic Powers, guardianship over the Nile: the Cosmic Powers are they who under Usen have overall oversight above the Kingdom Powers such as Odin and Ra. And much good did Ra do. It was he who there brought forth a tribal people into the semblance of a civilisation, and his name was a name of great authority and mission, hidden from all others without the need to know. It was permitted him to call into partnership lesser spirits, such as Nut and Hapi, in order to develop the land. It was not easy. Turannoi opposed this kingdom, as they opposed all kingdoms of Light, and Ra had to contend with Apophis, a mighty Power of rebellion. Ra became Egypt's first pharaoh in order to lead the mortals of Egypt into truth and abundance, yet in mortal body dwelt overlong into dotage, and was mercifully overthrown by Guardians he had adopted as his children, for they had seen his wisdom waning.

"They took his mission to new levels, though saddened were they by their needful rebellion. Ra had had also to suffer rebellion among his mortal subjects, to which he summoned the Guardian Sekhmet to rend and slay them until they learned repentance. They did, but Sekhmet in turn became rebellious, until by Ra she saw that a gentler life could be hers, that love was stronger than bitterness. Thus it was that she was redeemed to her true nature and became Hathor, the Lady of Love.

"Her redemption offered us, drinkers too of blood, hope—might we in time return to the Light as she had, delivered from our evil mood? Yet as queen of vampires I closed my heart to this hope, for to give up blood was to give up life, and hatred ran deep. Many a time I stalked the banks of the Nile, drinking my fill of infant blood, and hoping that I might be the one to vanquish the vision of Light, to drink the blood of the infant destined to judge us, for I feared love and light and death.

"Though I dwelt not there, our focus was on Egypt—a mighty power until snuffed out by Arab invaders under their prophet. Then it was that the kingdom of Ra closed its gates, surrendering its stewardship. So it was that I remained in the dark when eastern magi went with many servants to a beleaguered people within a ring of iron, not of papyri. What cared we for them, a sheep people too insignificant to bring forth the prophesied king? For yet we believed that he would come from Egypt, not from the despised and rejected, those acquainted with grief. But among them a child was born.

"Guessing his age at the time of their homage, the magi sought the petty palace to seek the child-king foretold by the stars. Local diaboloi who had beheld an uncanny light shining over his birthplace, finally urged the paranoid king to slay dozens of village boys within the expected age, just to be safe, but deep heaven sent the chosen boy into Egypt.

"And so we lost our chance to slay him, for wrong-footed we were unsure as to who he was and where he was. In Egypt I had joined the hunt, only to discover that he had entered under guise and had long left Egypt. The diaboloi—whom we had joined for the hunt—soon identified him in the land of the Sheep, but were unable to kill him. Indeed they feared him since his sinless authority outmatched theirs. They fled from him until they found a frail link in his followers. Then they struck with a vengeance, gaining a victory beyond their wildest imagination.

"My advice to Necuratu the Dark Lord of the Abyss, had been that unable to prevent the man-child's birth, we should prevent the man's death, and so nullify the prophecy. But against my advice the Necroi nailed their own hands and feet, blind fools, and the cross became a symbol of cosmic prophecy foretelling our ultimate and total defeat by the power of Light. Thus it became a symbol of despair for both diaboloi and vampires, a threat able to break the will of the weaker vampires, separating soul from body. But for most of us it was damning but not deadly. But..."

Admiral Ránpalan had interrupted the friends with unexpected news, which need not be mentioned here. That was many years ago, and we have moved on, and I now am old beyond count of days. Sufficient I think to say that many wonders and visitations lay before them on their journey here, and many times they would meet to enjoy the walks and talks of friendship.

I, Teppo, only child of Tariq and Wilma, have written this account from the journals of the good Fathers, supplemented by others of the Wise. Father Doyle was a lover of history and blest from his youth with knowledge from the Earth Files, as we now call them. Many morals he drew, and his own secret heart he revealed. His death was grieved over by Lilith, yet rejoiced over too.

We have prospered well. Our world, called Alpha Centauri Cb by Earth as was, we have renamed Tarikemen, honouring to the memory of he who was my father whom I knew not, without whose dedication none would be here. Many we honour in many ways.

The vessels that brought us here had been built to land and return, but arriving in this new world we dismantled our ships as best we could, burning our bridges once we knew that this world could sustain the life we had brought it. And, I who was conceived under another sun, expect not another hundred years under this sun.

She who was my mother has long departed to true life, as we say. Curiously only today an oldish child—his 300th birthday is soon—asked why we adults would not call her my 'mother'. I explained to him that 'mother' is a title of responsibility and pleasure, and that women who bear that title in mortal years, bear it no more upon entering the land beyond family trees, the land where all are free persons, where mortal seeds have become eternal flowers. So I call Wilma no longer 'mother', for she is no longer bound to me as mother—why call a *former* servant a servant still? Indeed her true name I know not, yet we shall meet again beyond all sunsets.

I hope I was understood, for it is good that while they are still young, children understand what Father Doyle —that beloved disciple of the Lady Lilith—taught us about true aioniology. One day soon I shall be as she who was mother is, for I am essentially of her kin, the human not the vampire. For the Simbolinians can conceive bodies, but not spirits. Though in the will of Usen I was given as a comfort to Wilma. The humanoid body of Tariq was but a creation of his kind. Therefore I am not of his kind though I am, in part, of his kind's creation. True, some special senses and skills I have in this life, but through death I shall go unto true humanity and be at one. My mind now dwells much on that great journey yet to begin, of which this life hints.

Besides his regular teaching times especially for his disciples, Father Doyle left behind much wisdom and knowledge in the form of the Earth Files taken from the Redcar Shelter in which he was raised. The shells of the starships retain some power from our suns, enabling us to read these files. By this we know much history and humanities with which to learn and to teach our descendants and descendants yet to be. Yet with the wisdom of hindsight and other bloods, we discriminate between good and ill, truth and folly.

Humanity's past is a mixed blessing. Family structures—surnames—we have rebuilt, and through marriage we have replanted family trees that grow well in this new world. The animals we brought—the ships were built to contain them as well as to supply food for human and animal kind—served us well and still do. No species was lost on the voyage, and those we allowed to wander wild have multiplied after their own kind, male and female.

Side by side with mankind dwell the sindeldi, no longer hidden. The hobs live at a little distance—preferring holes to houses. The Simbolinians have found renewed vigour and can fly free and orbit like moths with great joy. Their need for blood—a need I have never had—has ended, drawing strength from deep heaven with which they are in harmony. They visit us still in glad friendship, they who in the alliance found redemption and freedom.

At my last rise I was invited to the hall—sindeldi call their houses 'halls' and build them grander than we ours—of Ránpalan, the king who under Usen reigns over us. Thus spoke the king unto me: "Teppo, child of Tariq and Wilhelmina, greetings to my humble hall. Long I have known that you have record of times past, chronicling your people's time with The Beast, and of the Great Alliance that left its dominions. Behold, your world as was lies in the grip of ice, while your new world flourishes.

One day your people shall learn again the skills of flight, gaining knowledge from your records yet preserved, and understanding from the vessels that brought us here.

"It is your destiny that you will return, else will be returned—if I have read aright the eschatology of your people—for are you not to greet The Radiance on the borders of your home world? Are you not guests here while Earth's stage be reset fit for its final curtain? We will see. Yet however the future of your people shall unfold, your story is a pivotal story of the pantocrator, and it comes to my mind that you should send to your old world a copy thereof.

"For lo, it may even be that numbers of your kind live yet, sheltered mayhap in the dark caverns of the children of Durin, or mayhap those who return will have forgotten the story. Thus it would prove a blessing for the now, or for the future. But as to the why, I do not see clearly the mind of the pantocrator, save the prompting of my heart of what now is to be done. Assemble therefore a fair copy which I can send forth unto your people through the Stone of Skuld. Know this, that Kralvin of the Deep came unto me as we departed, bearing that which can send speech through time. Betwixt us and its answering stone on Earth, there is no time. And whatsoever a stone hears, it can store and speak it once to whosoever it chooses."

"So you can instantly be heard throughout the universe?" asked I.

"Only where there is another norn stone it can be heard so, although the stones choose the time: indeed the wayward Urd stone has been known to twist time so as to deliver a message before its time" smiled Ránpalan.

"Then is there not a danger that a message could alter the line of time, as if I went back killing my mother and father, and so, never being conceived, never killed father and mother, and so was conceived?"

"Child," he answered, "know that the pantocrator is beyond the mystery of time and space, though dwells also within his handiwork, even as an artist stands beyond and within their art. Be assured that he would allow no such contradiction, nor negation of his main strokes. Some change might be allowed to affect the minor but never the major. Consider the Ahab Arrow. What if that battle were refought with some change in time? In a differing fight some who had died might now live, while some who had lived might now die, but Ahab would still be doomed. For there is randomness in life, but also design. Other arrows may misfire but the arrow of prophecy will find its target true."

"But," said I, "what if there was no Ahab, what if the line of time had been so changed before he was conceived?"

Ránpalan smiled: "Where there is no problem there is no solution. Had he not been then there would have been no need for the prophecy and it would not have been. But he was, and was a problem to the cosmic plan and a warning to his people, even though grace allowed him to reflect, repent, and recommend, as he prepared to die. It is the cosmic plan which needed protection along the line, and your people of their freewill sometimes defied and sometimes defended it. Yet the prophetic flow carved its way to the sea of destiny. Prophecy can be interactive. The fixed steps—the cosmic plan—would always have been, no matter how others twist and turn it. As in chess, the supreme master will always conclude with a checkmate, though others force that conclusion to come by him coordinating his moves to theirs. But the important thing is not to understand the will of the pantocrator—though that is good—but to play one's obedient part in all willingness—for that is better. Come child, conclude your story, and I shall send it forth through the stone."

My story has ended. My mortal years shall soon end also, for I have now lived over 4,000 years and have seen my children to the sixth generation. I have read much of the Earth Files and learnt much of man's past. Authors I have read who in their mortal years spoke only to the people of their shores. Usen now allows me to speak to people of two worlds. So, O world from which we came, though we be now divergent, know now that it may well be that we will return to join you for the dénouement, and await us in blessed hope. Or else hear again, returners to a once barren Earth, the history of our leaving and hearken to Hamashiach. I Teppo, only child of Tariq and Wilma, have spoken, and will speak no more.

∞

Postscript

It need only be said that some quirk in the stone sent this journal unexpectedly back through time, an unlikely possibility but one which Ránpalan will foresee. Strange, that though Teppo has not been born, yet I know of him. Its heavy burden has fallen on my shoulders and has weighed heavily on my mind—what should I do about it? Doing nothing is not even to be considered, for that is to deny destiny. I could of course put his history into a time capsule and bury it as a seed in the ground to await its day to spring forth. After all, some prophecies have been sealed until their appointed time, and only the seed that is buried germinates.

But if I am merely to do that then why was it not *sent* to its appointed time? Yes, I could blame the quirky Norn sisters for delivering it to the wrong time—as the British postie delivers to the wrong place—but are they not under higher oversight? Does God blunder? It comes to my mind that the Seer of Patmos spoke of a time when the sealed should be unsealed, published globally. Am I being nudged?

In front of me it sits, this disturber of my peace. Over some weeks I have tinkered a bit with Teppo's quaint style and wording, for in one or two places the English of the post-technological future would puzzle our more technological world which tinkers towards the apocalypse. I have tried to keep within the spirit and style of the future writers, uncertain what else to do with it. This night as I prayerfully reconsider it, it has just hit me that if I hadn't trusted my friend—who in turn received it from a trusted friend of a trusted friend—I would probably believe it to be fantasy not fact.

This suggests to me the way forward. You see, on the one hand those who mistrust me will dismiss it as sheer fantasy, as water off a duck's back, and so do no harm by it. On the other hand those to whom I suppose it to be intended will be led by Hamashiach and do no harm—to you few I say, prepare the way of Adonai. Those in-between will read it neither as fact nor fantasy but as myth, unfocused truth, and as enlightened souls will draw useful inferences from it as helpful political trajectory and metamyth. In its time the truth will of course become clear to our race.

Yes, if I feel as sure tomorrow as I do tonight, I will simply go ahead and publish it. And it will probably be sensible to also bury—I will not tell you where—the copy that came to me. If Ránpalan's presumption will be justified—that it was then for possible traces of humanity sheltering underground, or for returners from Alpha Centauri Cb—I guess the manuscript will then be unearthed. My friend—each link in the chain is sealed in secrecy so I do not even say 'he' or 'she'—who felt 'guided' (their word) to hand this story to me, added that the person who transcribed it from the norn stone did so at the request of an ancient people who seldom come into the light.

As to who they were, my guess is that they are the race we call without belief, dwarves, the people of Durin. If I'm right, perhaps knowing the story in advance will lead them to pass on the Skuld Stone to Ránpalan, or is that one of those timeline contradictions that Teppo will ponder? Dwarves. I wonder if their safety is in the fact that humans don't really believe in them? I didn't. New truth is hard truth. As for the receiving stone—presumably the stone of Urd the Norn— I guess some kind of dictaphone is a fairly close equivalent.

Why did it come to me? I see that my own slow journey has prepared me for such a journal. Once I believed that all the 'gods' (and 'goddesses') of the peoples were idols, stones of demons, deceitful *elilim*. Now I have broadened—let our lord judge whether I have left the narrow way. Why are we warned against idols, the *façade* behind which some spirits conceal themselves? Could it be that they were simply guides of pre-Jerusalemic roads, pointing to the spiritual realm? Now that spiritual Jerusalem is built, roads away from are dangerous for everyone—remember the Good Samaritan?—and always were to those who were building earthly Jerusalem.

I don't deny that they can have value as dangerous roads *into* Jerusalem, yet they are doubly dangerous as roads *out of* Jerusalem. If the truth has set us free, why return to a yoke of slavery? And these idols—maybe demons, maybe divinities, but certainly not deities— do damage if they point to themselves. Misleading is most likely when it is the egocentric *diaboloi/daimonia* who inhabit the idols, but least likely when it is the unfallen spirits of deep heaven.

I don't know about you, but I don't put much faith in 'bishops'. In deem the idea to be a human construct, with the posts increasingly filled with infidels who would prepare the way for Ainet. Yet some have been much better Christians than I am, such as Nicholas Wright. Do you know, he said that *Colossians*, speaking about Principalities & Powers, picked up on Powers as squabbling spirits under pagan names, who "were created good, but got too big for their boots because we humans allowed them to." But, he said, on the cross Christ "defeated those rebel Powers, and stripped them of their ultimate power. Now he seeks to reconcile them...."

I guess that we could recall conflicts like Athena vs Aphrodite. Idols today, he said, are simply *too foggy*. Insights once useful for forward thinking are nowadays backward thinking, reversion. Some divinities were warlike, like Apollo and Athena. Might they be dim reflections of Yahweh the Warrior? Spiritual war is aggressive in the spiritual dimension, and our Christian fight is not against flesh and blood.

Other stories also carried messages, dim insights into Yahweh, dim but helpful once upon a time. For instance, Egyptian mythology contrasts a peasant and a noble after death. The nobleman's death was celebrated by pomp and pageant, but he failed the spiritual exam after death and was doomed. The godly peasant passed and entered into everlasting bliss. How many humble weddings have ended in happy marriages, and glam weddings in grim marriages, when some have put cart before horse? Good life is not glitz. Egypt—even a younger generation to an older—taught that we should not judge by mere appearances and status.

They had some insight, for Yahweh truly judges all *hearts*. Osiris would win the eschatological battle that would be fought against Set and his evil followers. Though *Revelation* gives a truer picture, both highlight the victory of righteousness. And Brahma was the first divinity of the Hindu Trinity that included Vishnu, who taught that devotion for him was better than even right living and meditation, though encouraging all three. C S Lewis also spoke of the three parts of morality, as did James of true religion.

In simple, Lewis once loved whatever opposed hated Christianity, yet through the ancient myths—*myth* as unfocused truth—he came to see Christianity as being what they prophesied, myth incarnate, true myth. Like him I have found the ancient myths to be colourful, enchanting, enlightening. Young children prefer picture books to text books, though the ink of poet or prophet might be much more colourful. Gambling arcades hook their bait with colours to eye and ear, to catch fish in a colourless sea—some churches do likewise, though their message might be little better than a gamble.

Wright noted that many Christians reject the idea of any good coming out of paganism—can any good come from Nazareth, isn't "a partial truth...the most effective lie"? Blessings of the past? Of course we should neither return to Nazareth nor to mere paganism (Dt.4:19), since the retrograde muddies what has become clear water, though the water is not always what we humans—who enjoy a little mud—would like. But muddied myths were not lies.

I still find it overwhelming to have had to rethink what human storytellers have told, and mistold, about the race we call vampires. Some readers of superstitious vampirism will indeed call *this* journal a lie. Kindlier souls will call it poetic licence. I shall say no more. And who knows, perhaps by publishing it my source will forward more stories to me—if I keep faith. For I choose to follow the wisdom of Ránpalan, who in our time remains hidden and perhaps hasn't yet moved to Mullaghcleevaun. He will believe that in the divine providence this journal was to be posted, and who am I to believe that it was delivered to the wrong address?

Cosmology

Being Types

- **Powers** (Type 2 beings)—spirits created within the Dynamic Bubble: unfallen Powers were Philikoi; fallen Powers were Turannoi. Three ranks/levels: Cosmic—could oversee a planet; Kingdom (unfallen guardians and fallen dunamoi)—spec ops or province based; Channels/Agents—tertiary helpers, foot soldiers, aggeloi (unfallen) and diaboloi (fallen).

- **Pneumata** (Type 3 beings)—cosmic-born spirits, created outside the Dynamic Bubble. Some were as powerful as Kingdom Powers. Disobedience diminished their power.

- **Psuchai** (Type 4 beings)—global-born spirits, such as sindeldi and humans.

The Pantocrator created Powers, Pneumata, and Psuchai, which could fall into disobedience. Powers outside the Dynamic Bubble could not change, but the hidden rebellion or submission of a few— systemic or superficial—could surface in real time. Phusika (Type 5 or lesser beings) he also created through intelligent code, but not in his Image. But to those of mortal souls, he gave images, dreams.

Spirit Kingdom Types

- **Necros**: actively against creator and creation

- **Night**: actively against creator

- **Grey Zone**: betwixt kingdoms, passively towards creator and creation, uncommitted

- **Dawn**: actively towards creator and creation

- **Day**: Hamashiachim actively towards creator and creation

The **Necros** is dark in heart and mind; the **Night** is dark in mind: in general terms, both are of the **Dark**. The **Dawn** is light in heart; the **Day** is light in heart and mind: in general terms, both are of the **Light**. The **Grey**, unsure and unaligned, is unconsciously of the **Light**.

Primary Characters

Ainet/The Beast
Alban, Fr.: Type 4
Cipolla, Fr.: Type 4
Doyle, Oswine, Fr.: Type 4
Draven: Type 3 (Dark to Light) Royal
Hamashiach/Huion: Type 4/1 ((The) Light) / Sui Generis
Lilith: Type 3 (Light) / Royal
Margery of Quether: Type 4 / slave-bride
Necuratu/Bent One: Type 2 (Dark) / Dark Lord
Odin: Type 2 (Light) / Royal
Pazuzu: Type 2 (Dark) / Noble
Ra: Type 2 (Light) / Royal
Rangda: Type 3 (Dark) / Royal
Ránpalan: Type 4 / Royal
Saradas Gormadocs: Type 4
Sunniva B-ELASIS: Type 4
Tariq E-DYDECA: Type 3 (Grey to Light)
Thor: Type 2 (Light) / Royal
Usen Pantocrator/Deo: Type 1 (The Light) / Cosmic Creator
Vidar: Type 2 (Light)
Wilma: Type 4

Books by this author

Theology

Israel's Gone Global

Israel's Gone Global traces salvation through the term, Israel. Was the covenant with the people-nation of Yakob-Yisrael, crossed out? How eternal is covenant? To examine that, we examine marriage. Can a covenant partner be truly divorced? Has Yeshua-Yisrael mediated a spiritual covenant with a spiritual Israel? Is evangelism of ethnic Jews needless, a priority, or neither?

No one could have everlasting life but for the cross, but has it always been globally accessible? Might any who die as Atheists, Hindus, or Islamists, make heaven? And is eternal life joyful? Is everlasting life fun?

Tackling the question of people who die in infancy (or as adults who never heard the gospel), we consider whether it is fair if only those who don't die in infancy get a chance of eternal damnation (if infant universalism), or alone get a chance of eternal heaven (if infant damnation). Does predilectionism make best sense of biblical revelation?

Opportunities to enjoy eternal life spring from the new covenant— reasons to rejoice. But what about salvation history before that covenant?

∞

Singing's Gone Global

Singing's Gone Global, briefly explores the background of singing, before and into ancient Israel. It examines the impact songs have on those who sing, and on those who listen, touching on spiritual warfare. It looks at how nonsense songs neither make sense to evangelism, nor to the evangelised, and asks, "Is there a mûmak in the room?"

Oddly some songwriters simply misunderstand prayer. Part two covers the basics of the trinity, focusing on the spirit in order to understand types of prayer (eg request, gratitude, adoration, chat), leading in turn to a better understanding of our heavenly father, our brother, our helper, and ourselves in Christ's likeness.

Next we look at some common problems. Part three focuses on problems such as buddyism, decontextualising, misvisualisation, and unitarianism. Diagnosis can help Christ's 'bride' to recover from suboptimal and unbiblical songs (Eph.5:18-30).

Giving a Problem Avoidance Grade (PAG)—an A+ to Unsatisfactory scale—in part four we examine specific songs. Weapons forged (Part three), the mûmakil can be attacked, seeking to save and be saved.

Subsequently the book concludes by showing how Christmas carols may be tweaked to better serve our weary world, rejoicing that joy to the world has come.

∞

The Word's Gone Global

The Word's Gone Global, examines Bible text (trusted by early Islam) and introduces textual critique. It looks at the Eastern Orthodox Bible and the Latin Vulgate. Did the Reformation improve text and translation? Were Wycliffe, Tyndale, and Martin, helpful?

Why did the New International Version begin, and why does it enrage? Why did complementarians Don Carson and Wayne Grudem, clash? Is marketing hype between formal and functional equivalence, meaningless? Which version or versions should you regularly read?

In English-speaking circles, Broughton wished to burn Bancroft's King James Version, yet many KJV proponents—think Gail Riplinger and Peter Ruckman—wish to burn all alternatives. More heat than light?

Grade Charts cover 30+ English versions on issues such as God's name, God's son's deity, marriage, gender terms, anti-polytheism, and various issues in John's Gospel. No, Tyndale was not 'born again'. No, John was not antisemitic. No, he did not disagree with the other Gospels.

∞

Prayer's Gone Global

Prayer's Gone Global, begins with ancient civilisations and prayer (the Common Level). Then it narrows into Ancient Israel and prayer (the Sinai Level). Then it deepens and widens into Global Israel and prayer (the Christian Level). Deity is revealed as trinity: Sabellians mislead.

Relating to the trinity includes the Holy Spirit. We should of course work with him, but should we worship him, complain to him, chat with him? Above the spirit stands the often forgotten father—oh let Jesusism retire.

Authority is another issue. Are we authorised to decree and declare? Is binding and loosing actually prayer, or is it evangelism? Is it biblical never to command miracles? Do we miss out on the supernatural which Jesus modelled for us, too fearful of strange fire to offer holy fire?

You can freshen up your prayer life—ride the blessed camel, not the gnats. Listen to Saint Anselm pray, and C S Lewis and 'Malcolm' discuss prayer, and be blessed.

∞

Revelation's Gone Global

Revelation's Gone Global, is a telling of John's future, as if by a then contemporary named Sonafets speaking to his church about how John's apocalyptic scroll related to their days, and about what was still future to John.

Encouragement is a big theme. Roman persecution was an unpredictable beast which ferociously lashed out here and there—what church or Christian was safe? But God stood behind the scenes, allowing but limiting their enemy, and messiah walked among the churches, lights to the world.

Victory lay neither with Rome nor demons, but with God, and with the warrior lamb who had been slain. Victory was guaranteed, and would finally be enjoyed.

Exhortation was given to believers, to play their part while on the mortal stage. They were to walk in the light, and not to let the show down by straying.

Angels of power, actively working out God's will, far exceed the puny forces against God and his church. His wrath was not pleasant, but could be redemptive until the new age begins.

C S Lewis' essay, The World's Last Night, is briefly examined to enjoin a calm awareness of the ongoing battle we are in, and the brightness to come when the king returns.

∞

The Father's Gone Global

Focusing from God as father, to the specific person of God the father, The Father's Gone Global looks at the biblical parent/child pattern from Genesis, through Sinai, and into the Church.

Abba as a new covenant word expresses deep filial affection even under deep anguish in our Gethsemane battles. Coming through God's belovèd son, it speaks into the church and into our lives.

Though to many the 'forgotten father', human parents/fathers should 'put on' God the father, and his children should 'put on' his son. We forget him to our cost.

Human applications aside, what is the Eternal Society? Is filial relationship modelled by God the son incarnate? Are we to be always obedient to our father and guided by the spirit?

Eschatologically the father will be supreme, but even now he is the one to whom the son points. Christian life should relate to God our father, God our brother, and God our helper, prioritising the father.

Renewal of the church is vital for our confused world, but renewal which downplays the father falls short of the good news which Christ created and the spirit circulates. May this book play its part.

∞

Salvation Now and Life Beyond

Salvation Now, divides the doctrine of salvation into the four main levels of common humanity, the old covenant, the new covenant, and life beyond.

A big weight is put on the term, Israel, as God's master plan. This too has four levels, meaning a man, a people, a new man, and a new people, respectively.

Various ideas of what Christianity, the new covenant for the new people, is good for, and how we get into it and best enjoy it, are examined, and a faith-based inexclusivism is suggested.

Everlasting life is seen as the ultimate goal of salvation, universal meaningfulness and love beyond all fears and pains.

∞

Revisiting

Revisiting The Challenging Counterfeit

Revisiting The Challenging Counterfeit, is an extended review of Raphael Gasson's 'The Challenging Counterfeit' (1966). Raphael was an ethnic Jew whose spiritual journey included many years as a Christian Spiritualist minister.

Today, when psychic phenomena captures the imagination and the bank accounts of popular media, it is useful to unearth the witness of one who had well worn the T-shirt of a medium with pride, only to bury it in unholy ground as a thing of shame and of sorrow and of wasted time.

Challengingly, his book exposes what true Spiritualism is. He had nothing but high praise for Spiritualists, and deep condemnation for Spiritualism. For he had discovered true Spiritualism to be itself a fake of true Spirituality, a mere Counterfeit that, in deposing death in the mind, enthroned it in the soul.

Counterfeit phenomena covered include apparitions, Rescue Work and haunted houses, materialisation of pets, psychic healing, Lyceums, clairvoyance, and OOBEs—to name but a few. This book surveys his exposé of Spiritualism's offer of fascinating fish bait, false food falling short of real food for the soul. Though it takes issue with

Raphael on a number of points, his core insights are powerful and timely, helping us to avoid—or escape from—a Challenging Counterfeit, and to discover true spiritual currency.

∞

Revisiting The Pilgrim's Progress

Revisiting The Pilgrim's Progress, is a re-dreaming of John Bunyan's most famous dream. An ex-serviceman and ex-jailbird, he found fortune, freedom, and fans worldwide.

This dream journey is substantially Bunyan's from this world, and into that which is to come. It is not a fun story, but it has lots of danger, and joy, and reflection on some big life themes.

Profoundly, sinners who become pilgrims become saints. But that can make life more difficult. One big question is, Is it worth it? One big temptation is, Turn back or turn aside. And if you see others do so, that makes it harder not to. Bunyan was tempted. And he discovered that not deserting, can lead to despair. But he also discovered a key to liberty.

Pre-eminently, it is a story of grace which many follow. Grace begins the journey, helps along the way, and brings the story to a happily ever after. Are all fairy stories based on heaven?

∞

Fantasy

The Simbolinian Files

From Simboliniad, a crystal planet long gone, came the vampire race, the wapierze, thelodynamic shapeshifters seeking blood. Most oppose Usen, King of the Light, so side with the Necros. Seldom do the Guardians intervene. These files, secretly secured from various insider sources, reveal something of what they have done, and will do.

∞

Vampire Redemption

Artificial intelligence, created by superpowers to save man, questions man's worth, and becomes The Beast. Escaping into the wild, many discover a wilderness infested by zombies and diabolical spirits. Who will help? Father Doyle? He's tied up with the mysterious Lilith.

Tariq? He's tied up with Wilma. Can the bigoted old exorcist deliver him from evil?

Radical problems can require radical solutions. But does man really need hobs, elves, and the more ancient of days? In the surrounding shadows, vampires and demons form an alliance, raising the stakes against Whitby and Tyneside. Powerful vampires live shrouded within Whitby, speaking of life beyond this galaxy. Is salvation in the stars? Is Sunniva, the despised woman of Alban, worth dying for? Big questions, needing big answers. Not even Guardian Odin can foretell man's fate and, as silent stars go by, one little town must awake from its dreams.

Though The Beast slumbers purposeless and undisturbed, in the far west a global giant slowly opens its yellow eyes and threatens to smother the earth in fire and ice. There is one chance only.

∞

Vampire Extraction

Bitterly long their imprisoned spirits lay, fast bound to Earth's drowsy decay. To the Simbolinian race, there was no hell on Earth, for Earth was hell, and Usen the cosmic jailer. Was it so surprising that as vampires they stalked Usen's children for blood? Most chose the Kingdom of Night, wary of both the Kingdom of Necros and the Kingdom of Dawn.

As queen of the Night, Lilith's story streams through the summer sands of Sumer, and through the green woods of Sherwood. It flags up both dishonour and joy, and cuts across the paths of Ulrica the Saxon and Robin the Hood, as tyrannies rise and fall in merry England. Bigotry seldom has a good word to say about Usen, nor about mercy. Reluctantly, Lilith examines what it means to show mercy, to show weakness. Wulfgar had enslaved Ulrica: is it mercy to let her burn; should mercy have spared Lona? Could Hamashiach turn daughter into sister? Could Count Dracula be turned from his madness? Has Draven really betrayed his mother? Life has many questions.

Tales picture ideas, letting us walk through the eyes of others to better see ourselves. This story exposes subplots behind common history. How these chronicles came to be written up is, in the spirit confidentiality, not for the public eye. What truth is within you must judge. Discrimination is a gift from Beyond, from which the words still echo: mercy is better than sacrifice. Indeed mercy can be sacrifice. Judge well.

∞

Vampire Count

Vampires were not always earthbound, nor are all evil, but being victims of Usen's Eighth Law, his Children became their fair game. Yet the Night Kingdom was divided: some veered to the Necros; some to the Dawn. Who was wrong; who was right?

Long ago one incited his people to racial violence against elven and human kinds. Ever he strove to be king of the Night, and unto Necuratu the Dark Lord he gave the dragon shape. He made war upon the ancient Middle East, even the Nephilim War. Against him the Light raised flood and division.

At last his own people, paying the price of his rampage, bound him in deep sleep. Yet the millennia seemed meaningless to him: even the rising of Hamashiach hardly disturbed his dreams. At last awoken, he and his brides stalked the hills of Transylvania. Only the fear of Lilith—and after her unforgivable sin, Queen Rangda—chained their bloodlust.

Dracula sought escape and autonomy. By cunning and devious means, he immigrated to London via Whitby. Pursuit followed swiftly, with a shadowminder helping a circle of human headhunters, though they sought the death of all vampires.

∞

Vampire Grail

Wulfgar is a vampire, a thelodynamic creature from another galaxy, now locked into our world by one called the Cosmic Jailer. He hides a tormenting secret from his queen, Lilith, which the Necros use as blackmail. She will only go so far with the Necros against Hamashiach—Wulfgar must go further.

Unknown to the Darkness, to bury Hamashiach is to plant the Light. From the buried seed springs life, and humanity must reimagine itself. Longinus turns to The Way, the nexus of the Seventh Age. His spear goes on a special mission to the island of Briton, where Wulfgar lives again.

Logres is centred on Avalon, but raises up Arthur, a man of mixed race, to carry its flag and to protect against the Saxons. But its main enemy is the Darkness, which ever seeks to extinguish the Light it hates and fears.

Finally, it seems as if the Darkness has won, and the dark ages descend. But does the Light not shine in the Darkness? Must Wulfgar remain in the Night?

∞

Vampire Shadows

Dark vampires, hidden within the ancient empire of Khem, fall out with the king who, stirred up by the Necros, enslaves the Sheep People. But Iahveh, the shepherd-divinity, is stirred up, and stirs up a hidden hero to force a way out.

Apprehensively the two vampire-magicians join the Sheep of Iahveh, on their long and deadly trek in search of a promised land. Can any survive?

Warily they ask deep questions. Is Usen evil, as prejudice says? Is he possibly a good jailer? Are his unusual regulations, meaningful? They risk ending up in death.

Neverendingly the Sheep's sorry story drags out in interminable peregrination. Weary of wandering, most would settle for some green pastures and untroubled waters. But as they well know, that would take a miracle.

www.ingramcontent.com/pod-product-compliance
Lightning Source LLC
Chambersburg PA
CBHW020246150626
46552CB00020B/531